Mything You:
A Brew of Stories, Plays, and Poems
About Myths, Fables, and Fairy Tales

Also by Dan Richman:

Farming in San Francisco

African Yamassee

Thursday, sold ?

Mything You:
A Brew of Stories, Plays, and Poems
About Myths, Fables, and Fairy Tales

Dan Richman

Cunning Crow Books

2014

First Printing: 2014
ISBN 978-1-304-82787-6

Cunning Crow Books
4229 21st St.
San Francisco, CA 95127
www.cunningcrowbooks.com

Ordering Information:
Special discounts are available on quantity purchases by corporations, associations,
educators, and others. For details, contact the publisher at the above listed address.
U.S. trade bookstores and wholesalers: Please contact Cunning Crow Books
Tel: (415) 647-4449, email cunningcrowbooks@earthlink.net.

To the great mysteries in the Universe.
And to those who welcome them.

Contents

Author's Note

I can come up with a dozen fancy reasons why a 74-year-old man would write a bunch of stories, plays, and poems based on myths and fairy tales, reasons serious and heavy. But in my case (and this book does have my name on the cover), the most truthful reason is - I love 'em! Still! In all these years, no literary experience has thrilled me more than when "Rapunzel," or "Jack and the Beanstalk, or "The Grasshopper and the Ants" were read to me as a child. No written words have absorbed me as much as when later, when I was supposed to be doing my homework, I instead poured over the "Tales of the Knights of the Roundtable," or "Robin Hood," or the ancient Greek myths. Nothing has enchanted me more than those stories. I suppose that means I never grew up in certain ways. Is that what you think? Just a little? H-m-m?

In any case, I remembered most of the tales used in this book, but also found some that were new for me in Bullfinch's *Mythology*, Robert Graves' *The Greek Myths, The Complete Fairy Tales* of the Brothers Grimm, and Aesop's *Fables*. I've briefly introduced some of these pieces in case you have forgotten the stories or were one of those terribly deprived children who never heard about them. And - here comes the Big Confession – I've also had the nerve to *invent* a few concoctions I put together using myth-like bits and pieces and hoped for the best.

Oh, and one more thing. Some of these tales and my treatment of them are light-hearted and some aren't. I hope you don't mind.

Warning

If you enter the forest as a child

don't expect to

ever leave it without a scratch.

↑

space

MAGIC

In the old tales, the homeliest things were sometimes invested with magic. A key would open an invisible door in a glass mountain. A pair of boots would project a person across a continent as quick as glanced light off a twirled mirror.

And this was done, not by electric current or compressed explosion, but by the forces rising from deep within the earth, from the organs of the Great Mother, which certain Ones, who concentrated deeply and at length, grasped and shaped and aimed.

The Earth had great influence then. It was not sheathed by the works of man. Great distances yawned between people, between cities — howling deserts, empty seas. And also profound forests dominating entire lands, from whose shadows slipped literature, and in whose clacking branches and rushing leaves, music suggested endless embellishments of itself.

The earth was naked then. Her influences, her musings, her terrible memories of being ripped from her father the Sun, of receiving his incestuous seed, of giving birth to Life, that insatiable child, and to her daughter the Moon, born dead, a pale bone-penetrated people, and they lived awestruck, respectful, distracted lives.

So that if magic rippled before them across a noon meadow, or flickered at night through a thicket like a fire-fly that would not fade, they reconciled themselves to being swept up by the drama. Or if they were ignored and passed over, they merely nodded their heads and went about their work in the wake of magic, a slightly trembling silence.

NOMAN

Very, very, very long ago when the world was new, there were three kinds of human being, and only one of each in existence - a man, a woman, and a noman. The man and the woman closely resembled you and me, as did the waggem, though it had a sharper face and more hair.

The three lived innocently in the same house, working the fields together in a golden light that was the afterglow of the recent Creation, like a sunrise all day long.

Then, one morning, the man saw the woman in a brook pouring water over her shining naked body and was pierced through his heart with a new and delicious pain.

Hesitantly, since history had just begun and almost everything that was done was done for the first time, he followed her around everywhere and gave her pretty shells and even tried a song or two in his hoarse voice to celebrate her newly-discovered beauty.

The woman became interested in the man's strange behavior and thought she would try it out herself. But when she sighed and trembled and said silly things, she found that the one who melted her opened heart was not the man, but the noman. Though the man desperately maneuvered to be her partner in all things all day long, the woman ignored him and insisted on eating, working, and sleeping beside the noman, giving the furry one the best cuts of meat, garlands of blossoms, and breathy compliments.

The noman couldn't help but notice that the other two were acting in a way never seen before. So not to be left behind, it began to imitate them as best it could despite its limitation, which was muteness. It could understand most of what the man and woman had to say, which was plenty. But though it could utter a few grunts and whines, that was all it could utter.

Nevertheless, the noman began to fawn and moan and roll its eyes and shower blossoms and pretty shells on the others until it made a discovery. If it was truly attracted to anyone, it was not the woman, but the man.

So there you have it. The man was after the woman, who was after the noman, who was after the man—the first love-triangle, and a perfect one at that, a three-sided cage.

The Creator, who had not yet become bored with the latest experiment and still hovered in the vicinity, looked down and saw that the human race would go nowhere without further modification. Obviously, one of these people had to go to force the remaining two into each other's arms. But which? All three were very interesting. But after all, the two chatterboxes needed to talk to someone who would talk back. Poor noman! But must it be eliminated entirely, this sweet, loyal, affectionate fellow?

A year later the Creator checked in on the project and saw the big-bellied woman walking hand-in-hand with the strutting man toward a beckoning future, the noman, now on four legs, trotting lovingly at their heels.

THE GRASSHOPPER AND THE ANTS

(From a long-lost childhood book) ⟶ *Itali* ✓

Green as a celery stalk,
and as fragile as one, the grasshopper
fiddled away summer in temples of grass,
halls of hot hours, kingdoms
of the sun, singing

Fiddle-dee-dum, fiddle-dee-dee,
nine-to-five is not for me.
I'd rather spread under a shoe
than work to death like you.

Meaning the ants,
who rattled by in red ranks,
sweating under tons of burgers and doughnuts,
the crumbs of picnics,
now junk-food addicts like us,
hooked innocents.

Fiddle-dee-dee, fiddle-dee-dum,
I'm a holy bum.
I'd rather end up on a hook
than punch a clock.

Antennae swayed toward the green one,
who though dumb, could carry a tune.
Then snapped back to work.
September, October, November
for ants are now or never.

Fiddle-dee-dee, fiddle-dee-doo...

But now a shadow fell. A leaf

15

parachuted,
then two or three.
Trees roared. The sun got something
in its eye. Teeth
chattered in our boy
as he hopped
oddly to the ants' door.

Knock. Knock.

Who's there?

The violinist.

We gave at the office.

That ain't funny. Can't hop,
for Christ's sake, can't sing,
nor violin
with wolves in the howling waste
that last week was Paradise.

Then, come in. Drink this.
But watch out. It's hot.
You want something. What?
And hurry. We're busy
with inventory.

Ants talk like that
in their delicatessen.

I want...I want...
some warmth. I want a roof, now that the sun's
shrunk and the stars are hard. I want...
I want...
to stay with you
as long as snow blows and not the roses!

Stay?
But what can you do?
How can you pay?
By check or cash?

I have no stash.

Then you scrub and clean?

I never learned.

Care for the young?
Care for the old?

I don't know.

Then books are your strength!
Numbers to the hundredth!

I live in the moment.

Then you're out of luck,
thin friend. Ice
waits. They say
it's not the worst death.

*But I can bow the violin
and sing poems grown in my green brain!*

As many times as you sang
when the light was kind,
we have your songs in mind.
Ants can memorize.
We don't need your voice.
In any case,
your fiddle grates.

You would expel me?

Completely.

But that's not the ending
in the Golden Book!
Ants are supposed to take me in
in winter
for the sake of art,
or plain kindness,
or at least
religion!

That was then. Now One Commandment
 is Pay Or Die, ethics
aborted. God
invests. The heart is a pump
in the breast,
nothing more,
nor less.
The prudent deserve
what fools divest.
There's the door. Here's your hat.
Watch your step.
Don't come back.

The lock snaps. The fiddler
looks out upon
two ends, the tomb
of December,
or warm soup
served by ants
who see the peril
in breaking the Old Ways,
in time to save him
and themselves.

Which shall it be?

Think it through.

The rush of history
might swerve
here.

THE KNOCK

After Bullfinch

*(Pluto, god of the Underworld, snatches the lovely young
Proserpine from a sun-filled meadow and draws her down
into the dark kingdom to be his bride. The girl's mother,
Demeter, searches the world over for her daughter, but
it's no use.
Proserpine is gone from this world. As Demeter despairs,
the world dies, since she is the goddess of all vegetation.
Finally Zeus, the boss god, steps in and a deal is made.
For half a year, the girl will remain in the Underworld,
but then she will reemerge, Demeter will rejoice, and
again the sun will shine and the seeds will grow. Thus,
people, you have one of the most touching metaphors for
the greatest miracle—the annual death and resurrection
of plants. Meanwhile...)*

At a knock
the mother unlocked the door
despite the wee hour
thinking it just might be her husband
who ran out on the family months ago
when things got difficult –
one of those guys.
And anyhow
momma was an open kind of woman,
torn open by her many children.

There in the dark in that terrible time
when the crops were dead
and the animals dying with their tongues hanging out
and the fruit-trees barren,
under too-bright stars,
bright like the eyes of starving children,
stood a towering woman in black
with a hidden face,
who just stood there saying nothing,

though the mother sensed no threat,
but sadness like a blossom's odor.

She sat the stranger by the fire
and brought her food she never touched.
She only sat without a sound
or sign for days and nights
till everyone got used to her.
The housecat found her lap. The kids
used her for their games
as tree, or target.
And through all of it she sat as still as rock.

But one night
long arms extended from the black cloak
toward the child in Mama's arms,
her youngest, a son.
And sensing no danger again,
Mama gave him over
and for days and nights the stranger fondled him
and made him laugh,
though never showed her face
but only her hands and breasts
when she nursed him,
which the mother noticed were as full as moons.

But she grew suspicious.
It was *her* son
 the guest was possessive with! And worse,
the boy who had been such trouble
with his blood mother,
on the stranger's lap
was a model child,
a smiler, a crooner, a content doll.

She crept out of her room at night to spy
and saw the mystery-woman,
still muffled,
lift the boy to the ceiling

as if to consecrate him to the beams and soot,
and saw the baby
who should not be walking at all,
no less performing,
balanced upright on a slender palm,
grinning like a small sun.

But one night the mother woke up from a dream
into a nightmare:
she found her baby lying in the hearth's flames!

With a scream she snatched him out
as any mother would,
though later when she could look back
without panic,
she remembered his giggles
and slaps at the flames that licked him
as if it were a field he lay in
and they were daisies.

But now her guest stood up
to the ceiling and dropped her cloak
and the hut was filled with light
and the trill of flutes. "Mother,
I am touched by your terror,"
the figure muttered.
"I am Demeter,
the harvest goddess,
in search of my missing daughter,
at my wit's end. Your son
soothed me. And in return
I tried to give him eternal life.
But you interrupted
and therefore he'll remain
a mere man and work till death
like the rest. Mother,
when gods offer gifts
no matter how unexpected
they must be accepted then and there or lost

forever."

At which the mother cried,
"But how are we to know?"
But the goddess had already slipped beneath the stars
that offer little logic
and less justice,
her every footstep changing soil into dust
as she searched the world pining
for her Proserpine.

DEATH IN LOVE

Death took the form of a woman for a while, and as Kali or Kore or some other bitter goddess or another, fell in love with a mortal man.

Well, why not, when you know or should know by now that Cupid and his bow spare nothing and no one, though the results of all that archery are often laughable or tragic?

And understand, this was a very pretty mortal man—golden beard, golden skin, golden eyes. A glittering coin in the world's grubby pocket.

And he played the mandolin and was a famous seducer.

One day Death, all white—clothes, eyes, skin—appeared to him on a bleak, bright road and declared her love.

The young man was terrified. And fascinated because she was beautiful, like a statue of marble.

He thought, "Wouldn't this be the prettiest feather in my cap? I mean...Death? How the others will envy me!"

And he smiled his golden smile.

And she approached.

But at her first step he wrinkled as if burnt.

At her second step he stooped over.

And at her third he bent in half and clawed horribly around for a cane.

Death stopped.

Did she actually look sad for a moment? Can Death look sadder than Death already looks—even for a moment?

"Dearest," she uttered, "you have stirred me as I was never before stirred and may never again be. But if I touch you I will kill you. So I will place you back into the hands of the Fates, who will decide how you live and for how long. But know that when the thread of your life is cut I shall be waiting for you with open arms."

Death took three steps backward, restoring to her love the bloom of youth, then disappeared behind an invisible curtain.

The young man, actually stupid and shallow, charms and all, strutted away into the rest of his life, carrying with him the important knowledge that at his last breath Death would be waiting to embrace him, as if out of the whole living world, he and he alone had been granted that privilege.

A TREE NAMED DAPHNE

A One-Act Comedy

From Bullfinch

(Alright, time to get childish. I mean literally, since I wrote this for children to perform and watch. Therefore, unless you are a child, don't you dare read a word of it!)

Characters By Order of Appearance

Daphne, a nymph
Mother Tree, the mother of Daphne
Cupid
The God Apollo
Lydia, his maidservant
A Squirrel
A Fawn
An Owl
A Robin
A Butterfly
A Raccoon
A Bird
A Rabbit
Various Other Forest Animals

Time and Place
Ancient and Mythological Greece

Scene

A painted back-drop of green hills, in which it would be nice to include a white temple or anything that would help set the mood. At right-stage is a stream represented by a bolt of shiny cloth flung down on the stage, perhaps at rear-stage draped over a chair as a waterfall. On one side of it stands MOTHER TREE, dressed as a tree, and on the other kneels DAPHNE, a pretty nymph in white, using the stream

26

as a mirror with which to comb her hair. At rear-center-stage stands CUPID practicing archery with his little bow at a bull's-eye target.

These above characters stand immobile and are bathed in low light until they enter into the stage action.

(From left-stage, enter APOLLO and his maidservant, LYDIA. APOLLO wears a splendid robe and carries a great bow in his hand and an axe in his belt. LYDIA wears drab clothes of the period and staggers under the weight of APOLLO's quiver of arrows and several other sacks. Both give the impression of having travelled a distance)

APOLLO

Lydia, have you noticed how quiet I've been in the last hour?

LYDIA

How could I not, Lord Apollo, when it's so unusual?

APOLLO

Yes, well... I've been thinking deeply, you see. I've looked at myself from every side and every angle and every corner, and I've come to an iron-bound conclusion...

LYDIA

You're good. You're very good. You're the best.

APOLLO

(glancing at her)
Well...well... That's it alright, but how did you know?

LYDIA

(putting down the stuff with a sigh of relief)
How? It's the same conclusion you come to every day.

APOLLO

(suddenly amused)

That's true! After all, every day there's more proof of it!

(counts off on his fingers)

I mean, not only am I the Ancient Greek God of healing, of athletics, of poetry, of music, of...of...

LYDIA

(almost bored)

Fortune-telling.

APOLLO

Oh, of course! How could I forget that, when every day mortals pray to me for glimpses of the truth about the past, the present, the future...?

LYDIA

Glimpses so vague, people are hardly the wiser for all that praying and sacrificing.

APOLLO

(lifting his chin)

I give them what they deserve. Mortals are famous for not recognizing the truth when they see it anyhow. So why waste a lot of it on them?

LYDIA

Elegant reasoning, boss.

APOLLO

(glancing at her sharply)

I hope you're not being sarcastic or ironic, Lydia. Nothing but nothing in the Universe is more tedious than a sarcastic or ironic maidservant!

LYDIA

(completely unruffled)

Fear not, Lord Apollo. I'm not being sarcastic nor ironic, since you're not paying me to be. It's not in my job-description.

APOLLO
(impatiently dismissing the subject with his hand)
Yes, yes. Now where were we?

LYDIA
Talking about you.

APOLLO
(beaming)
Of course we were! We were listing all the things I'm the Ancient
Greek God of. Did we mention music?

LYDIA
Yep.

APOLLO
Did we mention poetry?

LYDIA
Yep.

APOLLO
Did we mention cities?

LYDIA
Nope.

APOLLO
Ah-ha! Yet another feather in my cap! And I'm sure there's more. Did
we mention...er...er...
(snapping fingers)

LYDIA
(jabbing her thumb upward)
The sun? You know, the ess-yoo-en, sun?

APOLLO

(slapping his forehead)

Ah, dear girl! The sun! The sun! I almost forgot my daily job! How could I almost forget my daily job?

LYDIA

I forget mine at one second after five P.M., seven days a week.

APOLLO

And it has to be, just has to be, the most important job in the world!
Can you imagine what would happen if I called in sick one day? Why,
the horses would doze in their stalls. The chariot would sag in the
barn. The sun would simply boil over in a fury, popping and hissing
there in the shadows with no one to carry it across the sky! Oh, would
it fume, stuck, stuck below the eastern horizon!
    (sighs)
And no flowers would open that morning. No birds would sing. No
fish would jump in the rivers. No butterflies would flutter by...

    (wipes away a tear)

LYDIA

    (flatly)
It would stay dark.

APOLLO

Precisely! Until I appeared and whistled up the horses, tethered them
to the chariot, stowed the old sun safely on board, and hopped in and
drove it across the sky, just as I have every day since, since...

LYDIA

Way back.

APOLLO

    (slightly startled)
Yes... You do have a way with words, Lydia. The way a butcher
wields a cleaver. But a way.

LYDIA

I'm too tired for poetry. Your stuff weighs a ton.
    (kicks the bundles)

APOLLO

(loftily)

We all have our burdens to bear. Yours is to carry my arrows and a change of clothes. Mine is to light the world.

(suddenly excited)

And if that wasn't enough, what just happened, Lydia? What just happened no more than an hour ago?

LYDIA

You killed a snake.

APOLLO

A snake? That was no mere snake, Lydia! That was a serpent from Hell on the verge of swallowing the world!

LYDIA

So, a big snake.

APOLLO

A very big snake! And what did I do? How did I kill it? You must remember every detail to pass on to your children and on down through the ages!

LYDIA

(aside)

Children? I should live so long! How can I have children, when the only guy I love is a pompous ass who looks upon me as a beast of burden?

APOLLO

(raising his bow)

Do you remember, Lydia? You must! This is history in the making! I raised my bow like this, nocked an arrow,

(He pantomimes drawing an arrow from the quiver and placing it on the string, then draws the bow back full-length then let fly!)

(As APOLLO goes through these motions, the lights come up on CUPID, which sets him in motion. He too draws back his tiny bow, and before APOLLO can release his arrow, he pantomimes releasing an arrow toward the target with a loud twang. This arrests APOLLO and he lowers his bow without firing)

APOLLO (cont)
(to LYDIA)
Did you hear that? It wasn't I. Here's my arrow. Then who was it? Or what?
(he looks around)

LYDIA
(staring at CUPID)
Uh-h. I think I know.

APOLLO
(still darting his eyes around)
You think you know? Well, share it with me, Lydia! Share it!
(now spotting CUPID, who is staring at the target ruefully)
Why...! Look, Lydia! It's...it's a little child!

LYDIA
Uh-h, boss... That's no ordinary little child...

APOLLO
(laughing)
Talk about cute? And funny? Oh, this is rich! I just killed a snake the size of the world with my mighty bow, and here's this...this *baby* with a toy in his chubby little hand! Ha! Ha!

(shouts, with hand cupped at his mouth)
Hey, kid! Kid!

(CUPID turns toward him with some annoyance. LYDIA puts a restraining hand on his sleeve, then withdraws it immediately as if remembering her place)

LYDIA

Lord Apollo! I'm telling you - I mean suggesting strongly - don't mess with that boy!

APOLLO

(enormously pleased with his own cleverness)

Hey, kid! What do you shoot with that twig? Air? Leaves? Rain-drops?

LYDIA

Boss! Listen to me for a minute! Don't you know who that is? That's Cupid! Cupid, for Pete's sake!

APOLLO

(pausing, wrinkling his brow)

Cupid? Ah, yes. I've heard of him somewhere, but I can't quite remember his place in the scheme of things...

LYDIA

(aside, ruefully)

Tell me about it!

APOLLO

(shaking his head and laughing)

Well, never mind! This is good sport! Will you look, Lydia! Will you look at the face he's making at me! Ha-ha!

(shouts again)

Hey, boy! Whatever you do, don't shoot yourself in the foot with that thing!

(Now getting seriously riled, CUPID stamps his foot.)

APOLLO (cont'd)

Ha-ha! Look! The baby's got a temper!

(shouts again)

Hey there, baby boy! If you misbehave I'll take you over my knee and spank you so hard, you'll - ha-ha! - you'll run home crying to your mother!

(At this, CUPID angrily nods his head as if coming to a decision, looks around quickly until he spots DAPHNE kneeling immobile by her stream, then nods again with a wicked little smile)

APOLLO (cont'd)
(still shouting)
And you can tell her - ha-ha! - you can tell her you got your bottom warmed by the mighty Apollo, saver of the world!

(LYDIA groans and puts her hands over her face. Meanwhile, CUPID pantomimes selecting an arrow from his quiver, nocking it, and loosing it with a twang at APOLLO, who staggers back a step staring down at his heart and placing a hand there. LYDIA leaps to help, but again draws back shyly.)

APOLLO (cont'd)
(pantomimes drawing the arrow out and examining it)
Lydia, girl! He's...he's shot me! With a...well...what looks like a gold arrow!

LYDIA
(shocked)
Oh, boss! Now you've done it!
(Meanwhile, CUPID selects another arrow and lifts his bow toward DAPHNE. At this the lights go up on her, the stream, and MOTHER TREE, and she comes to life, combing her hair and humming sweetly)

APOLLO (cont'd)
(amazed, tossing the "arrow" aside)

But this is strange! I feel no pain! Instead, there's a warmth in my heart I never felt before!
> (CUPID twangs his arrow at DAPHNE, who springs up with a little cry, her hand to her heart. MOTHER TREE reacts to this by swaying violently to the sound of sudden roaring wind.)

DAPHNE

I've been shot! I've been shot with an arrow! I've been shot with a - yuck! - lead arrow!
> (pantomimes drawing and tossing it aside)

But this is strange! I feel no pain! Instead, there's a coldness in my heart I never felt before!
> (Still with his hand to his heart, not yet seeing DAPHNE, nor glancing at LYDIA, APOLLO looks around with a weak little smile.)

APOLLO

> (in a cooing voice)

I feel...different! I feel...like something new is about to happen to me...something new and...possibly wonderful!

DAPHNE

> (also looking around, but with alarm)

I feel...different! I feel...like something new is about to happen to me...something new and...possibly disgusting!
> (Now APOLLO sees DAPHNE and is stunned)

APOLLO

My god! I mean...myself! That girl! She's the most beautiful thing I've ever seen! More beautiful than the sun! Than the stars! Than...me!

LYDIA

Uh-oh! Now I *know* he's in real trouble!
> (As APOLLO takes a few steps toward DAPHNE, the nymph notices him and is repelled)

DAPHNE

My god! That man! He's the most hideous thing I've ever seen! More hideous than cockroaches! Than slugs! Than...than axes!

(As APOLLO approaches more closely, DAPHNE begins to back away)

APOLLO

What is your name, little angel? I am Apollo, Bringer of Light. I'm sure you've heard of me. Everyone has.

DAPHNE

I'm Daphne. A nobody. Nobody's heard of me and I'd like to keep it that way. Of course I've heard of you, but I was told you were the handsomest god there is. You just can't believe anything anymore.
(CUPID laughs wickedly to himself in the background)

LYDIA

(aside)
Alright, so she's cute with her little blond curls. But can she put in an honest day's work?
(As DAPHNE slowly backs up, APOLLO slowly advances)

APOLLO

Now hear this. I've made a decision. You, Daphne, shall be my bride!
(DAPHNE gasps)

LYDIA

(aside)
Tell me I didn't just hear what I just heard!

APOLLO

After all, you're the most beautiful girl in the Universe, and therefore a perfect match for me. I mean, I deserve it. Don't you agree?

DAPHNE

(beginning to back away in earnest)
No! I don't agree! You are a loathsome creature and I don't want you near me! I don't ever want to see you again! I don't even want to *think* of you again!

APOLLO

(laughing)
Oh! Playing hard to get, eh? I like that! The advance. The refusal. The chase. And finally - ah, yes! - the capture! Well! I say, let the games begin!
(APOLLO chases after DAPHNE, who runs off right-stage screaming)

LYDIA

Oh, for Pete's sake! How far is this going to go?
(CUPID prances forward to front-stage to stand beside LYDIA)

CUPID

How far? I'll tell you how far. Around the whole world, at least once. Maybe twice. Maybe more. That girl can run! She's run with the deer for years! I've watched her!
(LYDIA suddenly turns on CUPID, leaning over him, backing him up)

LYDIA

I'm on to you, Junior! Your love-arrow and your hate-arrow! I've seen you pull off some pretty tricky tricks in my day, but this is just plain nasty! Maybe you do need a good hard spanking! And I've got the muscles to do it! Want to see?

CUPID

But you heard what he said to me! He...he humiliated me! He hurt my feelings!

LYDIA

39

A-w-w! Did the big bad guy hurtzy-poo? Why is it that those who dish it out the most can't take it the most?

CUPID
Well, I'm accustomed to respect! I expect respect!

LYDIA

Say that ten times very fast! You expect respect? Ha! Folks either want you around or avoid you like the plague. It's all according to how you treat them. Or mistreat them.

CUPID

You're cynical!

LYDIA

No. I'm Lydia. And I've been around the block. I've seen what you can do. But what you did today takes the cake. Apollo can act like a big boob. I should know. But look at all the good he does. Under all that bluster he has a heart of gold - oops! Bad choice of words!

(Shocked at her own malapropism, LYDIA puts a hand to her mouth, giving CUPID a chance to rally)

CUPID
(wagging a finger in her face)
I just figured something out! You're in love with him! Right? Right?

(Now it's LYDIA's turn to back up)

LYDIA

Well, actually...

CUPID

Actually, you are. I recognize love when I see it. That's my business. Funny. I don't remember shooting an arrow into you. It must have been a long time ago. But never mind. Apollo needed to be taught a lesson, and I'm teaching it!

MOTHER TREE
(in a deep, slow voice, after rustling her branches)
Using my daughter as bait!

(At the first sound of the rustling branches, the FOREST ANIMALS enter quickly from stage-right. They cluster closely around MOTHER TREE and stare apprehensively at CUPID and LYDIA)

CUPID

(to LYDIA)
Why'd you change your voice?

LYDIA

I thought *you* were growling all of a sudden.

MOTHER TREE

It is I you are listening to. A tree, who happens to be Daphne's mother.

(LYDIA and CUPID turn to the tree in amazement)

LYDIA

A talking tree? The whole world's gone crazy!

SQUIRREL

Trees talk all the time! If people would just stop blabbering, they'd hear them!

MOTHER TREE

I warned her something would happen. I warned her she'd get in trouble in her two-legged form.

(LYDIA and CUPID approach MOTHER TREE)

LYDIA

What do you mean, "her two-legged form?" What other form was she ever in?

SQUIRREL

One-legged. A tree. She used to be a tree, growing right there beside the stream.

MOTHER TREE
I told her that two-leggeds lead complicated lives. They fall in love. They fall out of love. They argue. They worry. They...

SQUIRREL
I liked her better as a tree myself. She had soft branches!
   (sighs)
FAWN
   (in a little child's voice)
Well, I like her better as a two-legged person. She plays with me. She runs with me.
   (Off-stage, sounds of running, DAPHNE screaming, APOLLO laughing)

LYDIA
   (turning toward left-stage
Speaking of running...

   (DAPHNE enters from left-stage running and screaming, APOLLO right behind her, grinning hugely, both wearing huge Mexican hats and serapes. They exit right-stage without stopping)

CUPID
   (with his wicked grin)
That's once.

LYDIA
   (sharply)
Once, what?

CUPID
   (chuckling)
Once around the world!

(LYDIA approaches CUPID menacingly, rolling up her sleeve)

LYDIA

O. K., brat! You're time has come!

MOTHER TREE

They look at their wrist-watches. They work...

(This distracts LYDIA from her advance on CUPID. She
turns toward MOTHER TREE impatiently)

LYDIA

Who? Who? Who?

OWL

(delightedly)
Who-o-o! Who-o-o! Who-o-o!

ALL THE ANIMALS IN CHORUS

The two-leggeds!

LYDIA

(momentarily stunned)
I *get* it. I *get* it.

MOTHER TREE

But no. She had to "spread her wings." She had to "learn by
experience." She had to "find out for herself."

LYDIA

So, let me understand this. She was a tree?

(MOTHER TREE and all the ANIMALS nod together)

LYDIA (cont'd)

And she somehow changed herself into a person?

(MOTHER TREE and all the ANIMALS shake their heads)

LYDIA (cont'd)

Then, what?

SQUIRREL

She changed her into one.

LYDIA

(exasperated)
Who? Who? Who?

OWL

(with his usual enthusiasm)
Who-o-o! Who-o-o! Who-o-o!

(CUPID chuckles up his sleeve, vastly amused)

LYDIA

(losing it)
No! No! No! *I'm* asking the questions around here! *You* are answering them! My boss is chasing a girl around the world in a sombrero! I may lose him forever! Now give me a break!

MOTHER TREE

I changed her from a tree into a two-legged girl. I can do that, you know. Or at least I used to be able to do that when I wasn't so old. I could never refuse her. I suppose I've spoiled her. But she is my only child. You understand.

(All the ANIMALS nod their heads gravely)

SQUIRREL

And a lovely spoiled tree she was! Such soft branches!
(sighs)

OWL

She never woke me up when the sun was shining!
(sighs)

BIRD

She never woke me up when the sun went down!
(sighs)

BUTTERFLY

(in a whispery voice)
She never brushed me off when the wind was blowing!
(sighs)

ALL THE ANIMALS

I wish she'd come back!
(Again from left-stage are heard DAPHNE's screams and
APOLLO's laughter. As before the two enter at speed
from stage-left and exit stage-right, but this time draped in
bits of traditional Chinese clothing. They show some
signs of fatigue)

LYDIA

(aside)
Ancient Chinese proverb: What comes around, goes around.

CUPID

(wickedly delighted)
That's twice!

(LYDIA grabs CUPID by the scruff of his neck)

LYDIA

You're twice-dead!

FAWN

She's getting tired. I can tell. Her hooves aren't light-hearted.

(LYDIA again turns toward MOTHER TREE and the
ANIMALS. Distracted by her concern she allows CUPID
to slip from her grasp.)

LYDIA

And I'm worried about my boss too. I can't tell if he's laughing or wheezing.

ALL THE ANIMALS

Can't something be done?

LYDIA

You took the words right out of my mouth. What can be done! And who can do it?

OWL

Who-o-o!

LYDIA

That's enough out of you!

OWL

You-o-o! Who-o-o!

(LYDIA rolls her eyes. CUPID snickers)

SQUIRREL

Mother Tree, you changed Daphne into a girl. Can't you change her back into a tree?

(Cries of encouragement from the ANIMALS)

RACCOON

Yeah, Mother Tree! Winter changes to Summer. But Summer changes back to Winter. Can't you change Daphne back to what she used to be?

LYDIA

(eyes alight)

Oh, I like that idea! Apollo loves trees, but not as much as he loves pretty girls with little blond curls!

CUPID

He wouldn't chase a tree around the world - now how many times was that? Once? No. Twice? I think we're going for a triple here!

(As LYDIA gives the chuckling CUPID a dark look, all the ANIMALS shake their heads and groan with disapproval)

SQUIRREL

(to CUPID)
Don't you feel a little lonely right now? Everybody's worried about those two people except you.

CUPID

Who me? Lonely? Ha!

LYDIA

Ha? Then how come you look it? The bad little boy nobody likes at the moment?
(CUPID actually looks uncomfortable)

MOTHER TREE

How I wish I *could* change her back! But time has gone by and I've lost some of my magical powers. I'm afraid it's just impossible.
(LYDIA places her hand on her forehead in despair, then suddenly gets an idea)

LYDIA

(to CUPID)
Wait a minute! How about you, buster! You got us into this mess! How about getting us out?

CUPID

Well, I admit this has gone far enough. I mean three times around the world ought to teach anyone a lesson. Even a blow-hard like Apollo. And I didn't realize the girl was so...so popular...

LYDIA

So? So?

OWL

So-o-o! So-o-o!

CUPID

(uncomfortably)
Problem is...

ALL THE ANIMALS

So? So?

CUPID

(shuffling his feet)
See, I'm not designed to undo things. I can start something going, but
I can't stop it. That's in another department.
(All again groan. LYDIA again covers her face with her
hands. MOTHER TREE rustles her branches dejectedly.
CUPID raises his hands helplessly)

CUPID (cont'd)

(turning left-stage)
Wait a minute! I hear them coming around again!

LYDIA

I don't hear anything.

RABBIT

I do! That boy has ears like a rabbit!

LYDIA

This is getting out of hand.

CUPID

(frowning)

I really never expected them to last this long.

SQUIRREL

(to MOTHER TREE, suddenly getting an idea)

Mother Tree! What if we all helped you?

ALL THE ANIMALS

Yeah! What if we all helped you?

OWL

You-o-o!

MOTHER TREE

But how?

OWL

How-w-w!

SQUIRREL

Mother Tree, you said you had lost some of your magical powers.

MOTHER TREE

Yes. Too much, I'm afraid, to do any good.

SQUIRREL

But you still have *some* of your magical powers. Right?

MOTHER TREE

Yes. Some.

SQUIRREL

Well, what if you used all the magical powers you have, and we, (gesturing all around) all of us, did the rest?
(All the ANIMALS react excitedly)

ANIMALS

Yeah! What if!

CUPID

Well, you'd better figure out something soon! Here they come!

LYDIA

And once they do, they'll be gone again in a second! And I'm not sure they can *survive* another race around the world!

SQUIRREL

Mother Tree, do you think you could, sort of...stop everything for a minute? You know - freeze everybody in place?

MOTHER TREE

H-m-m. Yes...I think so. But just for a moment. I don't have the magical...

RACCOON

Squirrel, you're brilliant! For a squirrel. And Mother Tree, do you think, then, you could get Daphne to put down roots, right there by the stream where she used to grow?

MOTHER TREE

(slowly)
Yes. I think I could just manage that. But just. And what good would that do, a girl with little yellow curls rooted to the ground?

RACCOON

I'm...I'm not sure...

LYDIA

(aside)
I know what good it would do: make that girl look silly!

SQUIRREL

Look, guys! Let's have a conference!

(All the ANIMALS huddle for a moment)

CUPID

A meeting of the minds.

LYDIA

Never *you* mind, Mister Genius! We're all trying to clean up your mess. And it isn't easy! You're a real genius at messes!
(The ANIMALS cry out in chorus, slap each other's hands, football-style, and exit right-stage, running)

ANIMALS

Yes!

CUPID

There they go!
(whirls toward left-stage)
And here they come!

(Staggering by now, DAPHNE followed by APOLLO enter from right-stage festooned with nautical things - sea-weed, fish-nets, starfish, finny-fish, etc., APOLLO wheezing out a few laughs, DAPHNE screaming in a whisper. LYDIA rushes toward APOLLO with open arms, but halts uncertainly as before, her arms remaining extended)

LYDIA

Boss! Boss! Poor Boss!
(aside)
Poor me!

DAPHNE
(reaching the stream on her last legs)
Mother! Mother! Help me!

MOTHER TREE
(rustling her branches)
I will do what I can!
(The stage goes dark. First, the rush of wind through tree-branches is heard again. Then a minor chord played on a harp or guitar. Next, "lightning" flickers and thunder rolls and anything else happens that will suggest great magic taking place in the darkness.

When the lights come back up, there are APOLLO frozen in mid-laugh, LYDIA with her arms outstretched, CUPID looking a bit overwhelmed by his own handiwork, and DAPHNE standing prettily as before by the stream. At the same time the ANIMALS come rushing out carrying long white and red streamers. They dance around and around DAPHNE, quickly and expertly winding her with them, then jamming a white ball or helmet over her head, meanwhile whistling tunelessly as workers will do. At last they stand back to admire their work.)

SQUIRREL
No, no! That's all wrong! Those props are for "The Barber of Seville!" We've turned her into a barber-pole!

RACCOON
Well, I could use a trim.

SQUIRREL
You could use a brain-operation! Now take that off her! Let's do this right!

MOTHER TREE
(beginning to droop)

56

And quickly, please. This magic spell is wearing me out.
(The ANIMALS rip the ribbons and ball off DAPHNE and race off-stage)

DAPHNE
(in a stilted voice)
Mother, help me....

MOTHER TREE
We're working on it, dear. I think.

(The ANIMALS run back on with Christmas decorations with which they quickly festoon the girl. Again they stand back)

SQUIRREL
No, no! Wrong again, guys! Those are props for the Christmas play!

BUTTERFLY
This is fun!

FAWN
I want my present!

SQUIRREL
You'll get one at Christmas-time! If you're good! Now get rid of that stuff and grab the greenery! The greenery, I said!

(The ANIMALS whip the Christmas decorations off DAPHNE and rush back off-stage)

MOTHER TREE
The way I'm feeling, this may be our last chance.

(The ANIMALS re-enter at speed with branches and long green streamers, which they madly drape over DAPHNE until she is buried

maintain indented margin

57

in them, becoming indeed a tree. Then they fall flat on their backs, panting. There's a long moment of silence)

SQUIRREL

Whew!

RACCOON
(still flat on his back, panting)
Well, Mother Tree (pant!), did we do it?

SQUIRREL
(getting up)
Yeah! Did we or did we not do it?

MOTHER TREE

Why...yes! I believe we have! I believe my daughter has come home!

(All the ANIMALS leap up and cheer)

BIRD

And I'll be the first one to land on her branches!

SQUIRREL

No you won't! I'll be the first one to scamper on them!

RACCOON

That's what you think, Nutsy! I'll climb up on her before you get there!

(All the ANIMALS cry out while struggling with each other)

ANIMALS

No! No! Me! Me! I'm first! No, I am!

(With another clap of thunder, the ANIMALS stop in their tracks and look around fearfully)

BUTTERFLY

Wha-at was that!

MOTHER TREE

Well, I had to get your attention somehow! Don't you think you're all being silly? You should be dancing with joy instead of fighting!

(The ANIMALS look embarrassed)

MOTHER TREE (cont'd)

Now, my dear, dear Daphne! How do you feel?

DAPHNE

I feel...I feel...stiff!

RACCOON

(cheerily)
She's a tree, alright!

FAWN

(sadly)
That means she can't run with me anymore!

SQUIRREL

Aw, don't be sad, Fawny. You can sleep in her shade when the sun is high.

RABBIT

And you can hide under her when the - ugh! - hunters come.

BIRD

And you can build a nest in her branches when you need to lay eggs!

(All the ANIMALS turn to the BIRD and shake their heads)

ANIMALS

Uh-uh!

MOTHER TREE
Dear girl, it's only natural you should feel a bit strange at first. You were a two-legged for so long. But just think. Now you are home safe with me.

DAPHNE
Yes... It was so...interesting being a two-legged. But now I need a long rest. So much *happens* to them!

BIRD
I think all your experiences as a two-legged will make you an even better one-legged.

DAPHNE

That may be. I look forward to just staying in one place and growing tall. Just as long as I'm safe from that monster! Aren't I? Safe from that monster?

SQUIRREL

(wryly)
One would think.

RACCOON

(to MOTHER TREE)
Speaking of which... Couldn't we just sort of...keep him that way? (indicates the frozen APOLLO)
You know.

MOTHER TREE

Absolutely not! Why, the world would die! And anyway, I'm about at the end of my rope. No. We've done all we can do. Now we must take our chances. Animals! Break the spell!

ANIMALS

How?

OWL

Ho-o-o-w!

MOTHER TREE

Merely touch them. Touch them all! And I mean all!

BIRD

Just...touch them?

MOTHER TREE

That's the way it works.

BIRD

But I never touched a two-legged before.

BUTTERFLY

I have! They're soft! And warm! And sticky!

SQUIRREL

Guys, you heard Momma! Let's do it!

(The ANIMALS scurry about, gingerly touching
APOLLO, CUPID, and LYDIA. The three come to life,
stretching and rolling their heads, LYDIA still with her
arms outstretched toward APOLLO)

CUPID

O-o-o, my neck! I must have caught a chill.

LYDIA

Why are my arms up in the air? Oh! Right! (resuming her anxiety)
    Boss! Boss!

APOLLO

Now let's see. Where was I? Oh, yes. Ha-ha! Daphne!
    (stops and looks around)
    Daphne? Where did she go?

SQUIRREL

    (whispering to the other ANIMALS)
We don't have to tell him, do we?

RACCOON

    (whispering)
No, we don't! Then she'll really be safe!

APOLLO

Daphne? Where are you?

— *CLOSE UP* ✓

FAWN
(pointing to DAPHNE)
Right here! She's a tree again! I can nibble her leaves!

(All the ANIMALS turn on the FAWN in dismay)

ANIMALS
Sh-h-h!

SQUIRREL
Fawn! Why did you tell him?

FAWN
(in her tiny voice, beginning to cry)
Because my Daddy taught me never to lie! Wha-a-ah!

RACCOON
(putting his arm around FAWN)
It's alright, kid. It's alright.

APOLLO
(approaching DAPHNE)
Is it true?

SQUIRREL
Yup. Mother Tree and the gang changed her back into what she used
to be. To save her from you, if you don't mind my saying so.

LYDIA
(aside)
I suspected all along those yellow curls of hers weren't real!

APOLLO

63

So! My lovely Daphne is now a tree! Most unusual!

LYDIA

So I guess you'll give up on her! Right, Boss?

APOLLO

Give up? I should say not! Do you think I'm narrow-minded? (He reaches for DAPHNE's branches)
Daphne! Darling! I'll take you as you are!

(But as he tries to touch her, DAPHNE pulls her branches from him in   disgust, while all the ANIMALS groan in disapproval. At this, APOLLO steps back/ resigned at last)

APOLLO (cont'd)

Alright. Alright. I can take a hint. I'm not entirely lacking in subtlety.

BUTTERFLY

In what?

RACCOON

(irritably)
You know! Like all-of-a-sudden!

SQUIRREL

Sh-h-h! This is the big moment in every story!

APOLLO

I fell in love with you as I never have before. I pursued you around the world.

CUPID

Three times!

LYDIA

The brat must have majored in math.

APOLLO

But now I realize that, first of all, our romance was...well, shall we say, artificially induced?

(glances as CUPID with a wry smile, CUPID shrugging
his shoulders with mock innocence)
And second, that you don't want me, which I suspect was also
artificially induced, since how else could that possibly happen?

LYDIA

Your logic is devastating as always, Boss.

APOLLO

Yes...well. As I was saying...well, I already said it. Now a lesser
Ancient Greek god than myself might get angry at this ridiculous
situation and take revenge. With something like this!
(He whips an axe from his belt and brandishes it,
everyone reacting in horror)

ANIMALS

No! No!

CUPID

(turning away)
I think I'd better go and practice archery, right now!

LYDIA

Boss! Boss!

MOTHER TREE

(lashing her branches)
Sir! What would your mother say!

(But smiling broadly, APOLLO replaces the axe and
holds up his hand for silence)

APOLLO

But since I'm not a lesser Ancient Greek god, but Apollo, Bringer of
Light, and good, and...and... (turns to LYDIA, motioning to her to
help him out)
How did you put it, girl? You put it so well!

LYDIA

Good? Very good? The best?

APOLLO

Precisely! Since I'm all that, and more - now hear this! *Skip line*
(There's a short flourish of trumpets off-stage. Now
APOLLO raises himself up to full height and deepens his
voice, revealing his essentially noble nature, while
everyone else watches in awe)

APOLLO (cont'd)

Since you won't be my woman, you shall be the tree of heroes, and
remain green all year long, whether the flowers dance or ice grips the
world. Your leaves shall adorn the head of every great Emperor and
poet and playwright and athlete from this day on. And you shall no
longer be called "Daphne," but "Laurel." I have spoken.

(Once again, a flourish of trumpets)

BUTTERFLY

(tentatively)
Laurel...Laurel...

SQUIRREL

Laurel Tree! I like it!

MOTHER TREE

I like it too. Especially the last name.

APOLLO

(to DAPHNE)
Does that please you, dear girl?

DAPHNE

Yes, Lord Apollo. It pleases me deeply. I promise I will become a
tree worthy of the greatest of heroes.

(As DAPHNE bows deeply to APOLLO, there is general applause and cheering, APOLLO obviously delighted at his effect on everyone)

LYDIA
(aside)
Another day like this one, and I'll need occupational stress counseling.

APOLLO
(crooking his finger at CUPID)
Come here.

(CUPID wanders with great reluctance to center-stage to stand between APOLLO and LYDIA, where APOLLO puts his hand on his shoulder)

APOLLO (cont'd)
You've been a naughty boy, Cupid. But I don't hold it against you. No, I don't. Because I learned something. Do you know what I learned?

(CUPID shakes his head)

APOLLO (cont'd)
(genially)
In those moments when I was frozen to one spot, I learned that I *like* being a statue. And that's good, because some day, when my time is done and new gods take my place in Heaven, there will be nothing left of me but a few statues.

LYDIA
No, no, Boss! Don't talk like that!
(A general murmur of protest)

APOLLO
(holding up his hands for silence)

My dear friends, you needn't carry on so. Nothing remains forever. Everything must come to an end. That is a part of life, and if you love life you must love that too.

FAWN
(yawning)
Does that mean this play is nearly over? Because I'm getting sleepy...

(General chuckles. BUTTERFLY places a wing around FAWN)

APOLLO
(to CUPID)
I hurt your feelings, for which I apologize. On the other hand, you led me on a merry chase. So, I think we're even, don't you? I think our business with each other is finished.

(Peering deliberately first at APOLLO, then LYDIA, CUPID turns to the audience with an expression of utter deviltry)

CUPID
(to audience)
Oh, I don't know about *that!*

(LYDIA beams with happiness, while APOLLO stares at CUPID with furrowed brow)

RACCOON
Well, that was all very interesting. But what shall we do next?

SQUIRREL
What we always do when there's nothing else to do.

(Lively, rhythmic music erupts from off-stage. All dance, LYDIA with CUPID, the ANIMALS with each other around DAPHNE, APOLLO clapping his hands to the beat. Even the two TREES sway happily. Soon, though,

margin!

the dancers dance their way off stage. When they're all gone, MOTHER TREE leans over and hugs her daughter, as the curtain falls.

END

TWO ARROWS

(In ancient Greek drama, a Chorus would pop up here and there to review the action, or get emotional about it, or offer a moral to be learned from it. Here's a little Chorus thing for the preceding play. If you are a child you will find some of this redundant, since you've already suffered through the play. Just be patient and you might see something interesting come up. If you are a grownup and have skipped the play like a good little grownup, then you'll get an idea of the whole catastrophe starting...now.)

You would think
the god who drove the sun around the sky with horses
and gave us poetry and healing and cities
and stringed instruments,
who was famous for his pretty face and balls of brass
would know better than to diss
that dangerous baby, Cupid!

But no,
Apollo, Sun-driver, Killer of Serpents,
goes out of his way to mock the infant!
And gets shot in the heart for it
with an arrow of gold,
so that he falls crazy in love with the sexy Daphne,
who with a lead arrow and its poison in her
shot from the same itsy-bitsy bow,
hates him.

Does this ring a bell?
Look down at your own breast and you'll see why.
Those feathered things sticking out of you aren't bird's wings,
and you're no angel.
They're souvenirs of misconnections in both directions,
thanks to the juvenile delinquent,
the Ironical Kid,

71

Cupid.

But my next question is,
can you forgive
as Apollo did when Daphne
had her mommy change her to a tree
an inch beyond the god's reach? Then when
as an open-minded god,
not minding a little inter-species love,
Apollo bent to kiss the bark
of the rigid girl, but so potent was the lead in her system,
her very leaves
shrank back in horror from his lips?

The question is
in your darkest hour
could you make a grand and generous gesture
as Apollo did,
backing away from Daphne, bowing low, not
picking up an axe
as a lesser god might do,
but saying, "Alright!
I can take a hint!
Though you're not to be my squeeze,
I'll love you always.
And to prove it I'll arrange
that when poets
are honored, and athletes and soldiers and kings,
they shall be given crowns of your leaves
to wear on their heads.
And you shall be called Laurel,
tree of winners!"?

I ask again. Could you,
as pain grinds you
under its high heel
and every cell in your body cries, "Revenge!"
climb out of yourself enough
to manage such a sweet gift

that you come as close as you ever will
on the face of this savage earth
to the sweet
meadows of heaven?

Or if you believe the gods are dead,
as you sit alone
branched with arrows
beneath the echoing nothing,
could you be so sweet
that for a moment
you are the closest thing there is
to one?

I know I can't.
But I have hopes for you.

HUNTING SEASON

From Bullfinch

(Okay. That's enough fun. Now let's get serious— sort of. You'll see the worst sort of situation come about because of nothing more than a happy eyeball. And so here you have yet another example of just how ironic the Ancient Greek Gods could be. Not to mention Ancient Greek Writers)

What fools grown men
who have otherwise mastered
the tricks of dignity, prosperity, pomposity,
you name it, can make of themselves
at the flash of a woman's leg
or the swell of a breast
under a perfectly nice white blouse.
So pity the raw youth
hit by all of it
in one breath.

Actaeon
the boy prince
loved nothing more in the world,
besides the ladies,
than to roam the hills with his posh crowd
killing everything that moved,
hoofed, winged, or clawed,
living from one day of choked-off screams, blood,
and barbeque,
to the next,
a bit of a beast himself,
strutting around with the bones,
prongs, and paws of his kills,
he wore like dark jewels.

So how did the Great White Hunter,

stepping out of dense bush,
deal with a goddess in a pool,
as naked as a fish?

He gaped like the village idiot,
unable or unwilling
to tear his eyes off the holy honey
he had tripped over
as her girls poured water on her radiance,
glazing it. It was Artemis,
goddess of this and goddess of that,
twin sister of Apollo of the Sun,
and an ace archer like him,
who noticed her girls staring, and turning,
saw the grin
and reached for her bow.

Then changed her mind.

An arrow would have been kind.
But she changed him to a buck
with a rack like a tree.
And he ran like an expert
having chased them with his dog-pack
which now burst from the woods
sniffing meat.

"No!" he tried to shout.
"Down, Hero! Down, Spot!"
But it all came out squeaks and grunts
in the language of that beast.
They seized his legs.
They tore his guts.
And his boozy hunting buddies
roasted him on a spit
like good Boy Scouts,
and wondered what kept their chief
from a divine dinner,
while wiping him from their lips.

FLYBOYS

italicize

(With help from Grant's Myths of the Greeks and Romans*)*

"Is the old guy praying?"

Icarus was watching his father the scientist stare at the sky through endless afternoons.

"Is that how bad things are?"

Things were that bad. But what Professor Daedalus was actually doing was studying birds as they flitted through the air, hoping to imitate them.

What other hope was there? The King had clapped father and son in a tower, locked the door, and set brutal horsemen on the roads and spies on all the ships in port. That's how worried the King was that the genius inventor, throwing back a few shots in a tavern let's say, might blab the key to the Labyrinth, a vast underground maze like a subway system that Daedalus himself had built.

"What use is a maze," thundered the King, "if every Greek knows where to turn left and where to turn right?"

Though, come to think of it, knowing how to get through there s meant nothing unless the trespassing fool survived the monstrosity at the dark heart of the puzzle, the man-bull pawing the ground and filling the stale air with stinks, the hideous fruit of the Queen's womb, the scandal of the entire Empire - the Minotaur.

Oh, why did that woman have to lay her hot eyes on the bull in the first place, the perfect white bull splashing out of the surf, the gift to her husband from Poseidon, the sea god? And why did she come to desire the beast, for God's sake, enough to hire the great inventor, the world-renowned Professor Daedalus, to think up a way for her to impale herself on that magnificent, divine cock?

And why did the Professor outdo himself? The hollow, realistic cow sculpture with a hole under its tail, inside of which the Queen spread herself, drew the bull like a drunken sailor to a cat-house. The animal thrust through sticks and canvas into the sweet reality of the Queen, and soon the man-bull was born, the Minotaur - a royal horror that the King hired the famous inventor to hide away from the eyes of the world, at double his usual outrageous rates. Which he did, by

76

building the Labyrinth and imprisoning the Minotaur in its darkest center.

It all worked like a charm. The Queen, for once in her life, was sexually satisfied. The bull too. And the product of this grotesque coupling was forever hidden away from the sun.

Oh, why, why this whole, weird business?

The priests were quick to answer. "It was, of course, the work of the gods in their infinite wisdom. Yes, yes, the deities do work in mysterious ways. But they know exactly what they are up to. You'd realize that if you could only see the big picture, if you could only live long enough to see the glorious outcome of what at the moment seems disastrous."

Thus priests earn their living.

But Daedalus merely shrugged his shoulders at the insane lengths to which lust will drive us. He had left that stage of life behind a long time ago. And anyway, he was more of a how-man than a why-man. Why the world was as it was concerned him infinitely less than coming up with ways of dealing with the way the world was. That was his business, the business of the inventor.

The thing to be dealt with at that moment was his imprisonment and that of his tender son. And the rather desperate solution was to fly to freedom!

Daedalus and Icarus spent a month collecting the feathers of resident pigeons and gluing them with candle-wax to skeletal lattice-work carefully split from bed frames. Another month they spent leaping off chairs and flapping the new wings, which only sent them crashing to the floor.

But Daedalus looked to the birds again for answers. It struck him that he and Icarus needed to become like them in every possible way. He intuited that the birds' minds were uncluttered with the thoughts that tumbled endlessly through his own head and that of Icarus, and so the two began rigorous mind-cleansing exercises.

In time Daedalus came to realize what did dwell in the minds of birds – other birds. That would explain the amazing ability of flocks of thousands to turn and dive and soar in perfect unison. Their mental clarity allowed birds to be telepathic! So father and son learned to concentrate on each other in order to become a flock of two. They reached a point where they could anticipate each other's words and actions, and in fact, hardly needed to speak out loud at all to make their thoughts known.

And finally it was young Icarus who suggested the obvious. Since the birds were known for weighing next to nothing, he and Daedalus had better starve themselves to skin and bones, which they did.

Thus father and son became as light as feathers in both mind and body, and at last succeeded in flying around their rooms like huge, bumbling insects.

One dawn they dropped hand-in-hand from the tower's window until the air filled their beating wings and they shot over the gaping mouths of the King's guardsmen toward the million-mirrored sea.

The bleak beach of Crete retreated behind their heels as if a rough rug were dragged away. They were flapping in the void between the hard sea and the sun's high inferno.

Daedalus had warned the jubilant boy to fly at medium height, safe from both hooked wave crests and the sun's fury, not unlike the conservative advice given by many another anxious father to his wild child.

But this myth is as much about heedless youth as it is about science and its ironies or the impertinence of mere mortals.

The moment Daedalus caught the scent of cut grass and spied green hills crowned with white sheep rising from the sheen of the sea, he looked back to croon encouragement to Icarus, to tell him they were home. He saw nothing.

His beloved boy, enchanted by gadgetry, drunk on altitude, stupefied by delusions of grandeur – of divinity, even! - had already flung himself toward the sun, at the moment the only thing in the universe as glorious as himself in his estimation, had already had the feathers on his shoulders plucked one by one from the sun-melted wax by Gravity's rough hand, had already felt the sea snap shut above him as he sank to oblivion.

Daedalus named that place for drowned Icarus, then went on to live for many more crammed years of inventions, fame, pouches of silver. But never once did he feel as close to another human being as when he and his son became a flock of two.

ERYSICHTHON

from Bullfinch

(Upon first reading this tale, I immediately thought of a particularly greedy corporate raider, who fifteen or twenty years ago snatched up an old lumber company in Mendocino County, California, and clear-cut miles of ancient redwood trees to pay back debts. But now I see that this parable applies just as well to anyone who rapes the earth for money. Petrochemical corporations, for example.)

That old Greek, Erysichthon,
besides having an unpronounceable name,
was one of those rich guys
who wanted more, more, more.
Sound familiar?
So he clear-cut a forest
to extract every drachma,
leaving a junkyard of stumps,
branches piled like Pick-up-Sticks,
and dying leaves,
plus a lot of baffled
wildlife sniffing around the wreckage.

Rich guys like him
do that sort of thing.
Just watch 'em.

But when he reached a certain glade
and ordered his servants in with axes
they objected saying, "Master,
we know the danger in saying No
to a hot-shot like yourself.
But this grove is sacred

to Ceres
goddess of grain
who keeps our children's
bellies full. Moreover,
these trees have nymphs in them
who are her nuns,
whose lives begin and end
in these trunks.
So, dock us! Cut our wages!
Do anything,
but not this!"

But with a sneer that could kill at a distance, a long
long distance,
Mister Selfish
snatched up an axe
and chopped at an oak as old as the world
whose leaves were a swaying fragrant heaven,
that bled
blood, and cried in a woman's voice as it toppled.
The grove followed.
Every tree.
Night fell too.

Ceres
furious
rose like a moon from fields of corn
and called on her opposite,
Famine, to take revenge
on the son-of-a-bitch.

Into his bed she slipped,
this opposite of Ceres,
grim and slim and sinister,
a twisted sister,
so to speak.

Clasping him in her wasp's wings,
her mouth to his,

she breathed ill wind in him
so that he rose up ravenous.
Ate everything.
Sent out for more
Ate that.
Sold all he had - land,
house, and last, daughter,
a gentle flower,
to kill the hunger.

But nothing filled the void in him,
the emptiness of the soulless,
till gaunt, penniless,
hungrier than ever,
he turned to the only meat in sight,
his feet, crotch, heart, brain,
so that only his mouth remained,
his essence.

HELEN

(We've all heard of the Trojan War, the Trojan Horse, etc. But do we all know that this little girl was the cause of it?)

Believe me,
it wasn't only her face that launched a thousand ships.
Every inch of her swelled and melted
like moonlit surf.
Only where the ocean is frigid,
she was hot.

And no wonder.
Her mother Leda was so perfect bathing naked,
- such a wet and shining pearl! -
that Zeus, the boss god,
interrupted his busy schedule
to sneak out on his wife in a swan disguise,
(who's going to notice a huge bird
tip-toeing out the back door?) then sailed down to rape the bathing
beauty,
his wings beating winds.

And out of that cloud of feathers the girl was born.

Menaleus, you greybeard,
you were lucky enough to marry the maid,
and dumb enough to have young Paris over.
They didn't name the city for this boy for nothing.
In his young studly way he was as golden as Helen.

Menaleus, dim husband,
were you blind to the tunnel
that opened between the liquid children?
Were you deaf to the sudden beat of hearts
becoming drums?

82

Then you couldn't have heard the wheels turning in Heaven
arranging the war that tore the ancient world
that gave poets something to write about forever,
when the boy stole the girl.

ACHILLES

(I'm sure you recall that he was 99% impervious to swords, spears, arrows – anything you cared to throw at him. Something like a walking tank. The only vulnerable place on him was his heel. Well, his mother had to hold on to something when she dipped her baby in the transformative River Styx, didn't she?)

He never wore the necktie of fear
nor the hat of doubt. Nor did he sit in the puddle
of pettiness. Nor did he whine about taxes and wives and the newest
immigrants.
In this way he was different from us working stiffs.
For Achilles, all was a high cold plain
where he fought in the gaze of the gods
and won
and after drank wine with his men. Or lost
at last, as everything does, to watch his blood
sink down through the stones like a stream with an end.
All he did with his heart, soul, mind,
and back he bent up toward Olympus.
So too he was different from us. But in this
he was similar: his weakness
hung beneath his waist.

THE WEDDING

The bride burned through her dress.
The groom couldn't wait for the guests to leave
so that he could get to where the fire started.
Her mother and his mother cried.
Their fathers loosened their ties
and eyed each other,
recognizing themselves
in disappointing mirrors.
And Grandpa and Grandma watched the dancers
with one eye, the other
already opening dreams.

While all along the stranger in the corner
illuminated everything,
filling the house with a scent as sweet as anyone
had ever known.
No one could keep their eyes off it for long.
All knew it was a god
but were not sure which
nor why it had chosen to invite itself.
Was it here to grant immortality to anybody?
Or to steal the bride? Or the groom?
Or just to get drunk and dodge
divinity for two or three hours
of jokes and chit-chat
with the riff-raff?

GIANTS

We might feel some sympathy for the ancient giants, though they did eat people, though they did terrify children with their stompings and loomings and horrible faces, because we understand that the giants were victims of relativity. At one time they were the norm, until an Ice Age or a Flood or the sadistic kiss of a comet came along to cut history in two like a worm, both parts wriggling, when the Human Race was born.

Then they were monsters. And worse, the lice who bustled about their feet became increasingly more clever than they, and drowned them and burned them and toppled them from great heights, arms and legs pumping, huge falling bodies digging small valleys, people those days having less empathy for giants, when giants actually breathed the same air as they.

But more important than all this: Is the battle of big and small settled forever?

The giants in the old tales are gone. But aren't we becoming them, with our appetites that devour the world and our children towering over us?

We'll know when the next axe cuts history, swung by an as-yet-unknown arm, and a new race is born to trip us at the heels and turn us around and around, huge and stupid.

Or are they already swarming?

Look in the microscope.

JACK AND THE BEANSTALK

(Well, I've had about enough of the Ancient Greeks for now. Haven't you? How about the Middle Ages? Or the Outer Edges? For instance, here we have young Jack who breaks his impoverished mother's heart, when instead of selling their only cow for much-needed food, he trades it for a single bean. But he plants it outside their hovel, and overnight it grows so high it disappears into the clouds. Genetically altered, do you think?)

I've planted many a bean
but never did one of them grow
a mile high,
as did his, for which
he traded his hungry mother's only cow
to a slick
little bull-shitter.

Or was it an angel
with an angle?

Or a demon with a scheme.

I ask because
the kid climbs the vine
as kids will,
into a sky kingdom –
something like heaven
but with no God,
just a giant on the throne
with a sack of diamonds,
gold-laying hen,
and best of all,
since music is magic,
a harp that sings
like the wind in pines, or
if you prefer, like

Uncle Mike with a six-pack
but on command,
a sort of FM.

Jack steals all this and beats it.
And the giant slob
slides down the vine
in pursuit
from his dream of life
into the nasty
little Medieval hell
of kings, cut-throats,
religious fanatics,
plus peasants.

Being one of them,
Jack is acquainted with murder.
"Do bring me the axe, mother!"
cries he,
then chops and the vine
falls with a thud
including the dud
whose neck Jack steps on
to the applause of millions
of bedtime children
who learn exactly what
from this legend?

THE WOLF

(Do you realize how often we see the plot of "Little Red Riding Hood" unfold before our eyes? Why, just about every time we watch a TV crime drama! A predatory male lures a pretty young thing by disguising his true nature. As did the Wolf in the old fairy-tale, by dressing up as Little Red's grandmother. He's about to eat her when the Woodman—or TV cop— steps in and rescues her at the last minute.)

Since you know the forests were cut down to feed the Industrial Revolution, why are you so skeptical of the wolf's ability to fool young Red Riding Hood by the art of disguise, though she had spent years on the knee of the old grandmother, peering up into her face? He had frantically studied one step ahead of the woodman's axe, is all, the will to live so furious - mosquitoes at the North Pole, bacteria in the stratosphere, life whipping on and off one persona after the other before the rumbling wheel of death, with its sprockets and knobs and decapitating blades.

And why do you doubt that after the woodman beheaded the wolf he soon married Ms Hood and they became one of those deeply hip European couples we see stalking airports with their sculptured hair, pungent leather jackets, hundred dollar jeans, and pointy shoes, who know where to eat, what to say, and whom to snub with a cold confidence we can only dream about as we wander through the advertising in *The New Yorker*? Could they have survived the Euro and Big Mac in dirndls with grass in their hair?

Change, therefore, or die.

And so prepare yourself for the possibility of the wolf, handicap notwithstanding, breathing through his throat let's say, becoming himself a member of the icy glitterati, changing a tail's-length before the falling trees into a rabid devotee of radical diets, Ray-Bans, and cosmetic surgery.

OLD BALDY

(From Bullfinch. The original story offered a simple moral, I guess: if you try to please everyone, you end up with nothing yourself. But I couldn't resist updating and twisting it. I hope you'll forgive me.)

The gentleman takes a wife, not once but twice,
simultaneously. He's frisky
and has the money to feed three mouths
and then some if there's multiplication.
But there's a hitch. The second
is a generation younger than the other.
Apres sex, athletic and antiseptic,
the girl reaps the white hairs from his sweaty head
like lilies from a hill,
so as to slip him through her gang of babes and dudes
in the guise of a slightly more mature stud.
But the old woman seeks and plucks his black hairs
so that her head won't glow like snow
alone beneath the moon.
Now the old goat is as bald as a rock in the cold,
the hot topic of an entire town,
the joke in a hundred bars and nail-salons.

Yet our hero smiles on the bus
as he commutes home from his investments.
His baby is happy with his noggin
since shaven scalps, SS-style,
are hip with those born since 1971.
And the old lady gets hot with a pale skull.
For her, death and sex blur.

THE SWAN WING

Suggested by the Grimms' tale

The seven swans whistled down around their aromatic, bloody-handed sister. They needed the seven sweaters she was to have knit out of thorn-fanged rose-bushes to restore them to human form before the deadline, changed as they were by an ironic god with unfathomable motives. One by one they pulled on the cruel clothes - first, the eldest, the brilliant physicist, and then the man of business, followed by the slender real-estate speculator, then the local politician, the policeman, the dentist. All pulled on their scratchy sweaters. And all sprang back to what they were, merely grinning about the interruption in their life's momentum. All clapped each other on the back. Except the seventh brother, the youngest, who stood before the still-furiously knitting sister, anxiously, since the minute-hand was casting its shadow on twelve midnight and she had not yet completed the second sleeve of the final sweater, he finally jerking it out of her pain and drawing it on himself as the clock struck.

And there he stood, unlike the others, not restored to human wholeness, but with one wing of a swan instead of a right arm, one hopeless wing of white feathers and hollow bones, dooming him to the edge of the normal world to flap his one wing in an endless, futile attempt to fly. Which suited him fine in the end, since before the spell he was a poet straining impossibly toward perfection, and is still. And is still the only one of the brothers who finds the time to kiss the sister's hands every day for the rest of her haunted life, while keeping one ear cocked for the clearing of the god's throat, whose gestures are as perfect as a wasp's.

THE PROLETARIAT

(I had been reading about the noble Knights at Arthur's Roundtable, but having been a working man for much of my life, I couldn't help thinking about those people back then.)

The Squire followed on foot as best he could.
The heavy shield bent his arm.
The sword snagged his shoes.
The sweat soaked his shirt.

The Knight ahead rode lightly
brightly in the morning light, his head
filled with silvery
chivalry, and a gold crown,
and flapping flags in flowing fields.

Then the castle rose to meet them
out of the Knight's own
property, the Princess
at the parapet
also his.

Son of a bitch! the Squire thought,
slipping in fresh
horse shit.
I'll be doing this for the rest of history!

THE PRINCESS AND THE PEA

*(Suggested by a bedtime story read to me from, I think,
something called* The Golden Book.*)*

You know as well as I do
no girl could feel a pea
through twenty mattresses.
Nor an apple, for that matter.
It never happened. Or if it did,
it was a set-up from the get-go. In this scenario
the "Princess" is a ruthless opportunist.
Born to trash in a trailer,
sworn to leave them behind,
she peddles hers
to anyone on a higher rung.

Given cinematic bones
and the will of a wasp,
by intense study and hard schmoozing
she learns the walk, drawl, and insouciance
of the Upper Classes.
She becomes, in other words,
dangerous,
ascending through a thousand men
by stepping on them.

Now the ultimate test! Her shot at the top!
A royal bride must be as sensitive
as a fly! There she is,
perched on twenty mattresses
upon a pea.
She writhes around in a skimpy nightie.
She arches herself like a snake,
and having melted the secret out of a sergeant, moans
"My back! My back!
Is there no more comfortable bed in the Kingdom?"
And of course the king's son shows her one.

THE OLD KING

The old king leaned on a cold stone windowsill, his white head heavy on his hand, weighed down by the crown on his head, but also by the recent disappearance of his only child, his golden daughter, the sole female in his life since the death of the Queen.

He stared with red eyes across the worn and dying November fields toward the wall of the forest, into which, many said, crossing themselves, the girl had been lured by a half-man, half-beast, the very devil with wind-instruments, who had bemused her with his imitations of every know bird-call, operatic melodies, the songs of the wind itself.

She had ever baffled him, this hard girl. Brought up by tutors from busy, far-off lands to the west, she had shown no interest whatsoever in the trappings and responsibilities of royalty, nor in the melodramatic history of their family, nor in hawking, nor hunting, nor riding to hounds, nor weaving, nor handsome young men, nor for that matter, pretty young women, nor philosophical discourse, not to mention gossip with twittering maid-servants.

Only when she asked about the number of pounds of gold in his tower, or mused about the potential value of his timber, or calculated the profits to be made from the increased sweat of the peasants, did her eyes light up in a way that disturbed him, that haunted his dreams. He had never seen a light like that before, except perhaps in the eyes of a wolf too close to the flocks.

He stared into the forest trying to untie its endless knots until he died, fortunately, before he learned that his daughter had indeed been lured into the trees, but not by a satyr, nor man-of-the-woods, nor musician, but by a perfect salesman, a master of silken words and devious games, who shared the girl's fascination for coins clinking in little leather bags.

Yes, it was the clinking that drew her into the forest after him.

But then through it into the future, where kings and queens and forests and fields and peasants and pigs and all, all would be squeezed by people like them and their children's children onto white paper, where numbers march like black insects.

CAMELOT IT AIN'T

Suggested by the many versions of the story of King Arthur

(Merlin, of course, was the wizard who took the young Arthur under his wing, and who advised him well throughout his kingship to the end of his glorious days. Where are they now that we need them oh so badly?)

Finding a future king in the boy
Merlin took Arthur out of school and with his magic
had him swim with fishes in the pond,
fly with starlings through the city streets
run with packs of wolves in snow
and with the deer as well,
so that the boy would know the terror of the prey
and not just the passion of the chase.
Because the wizard knew
before else the human was a beast
and if the king would rule them wisely
he must first sniff the anus.

Now our leaders live their minutes
with ties against their windpipes
or straps around their wombs and breasts
in office buildings with sealed windows
and in tight jets and armored limos.
And each day they fly further
from the fin, the tooth, the fur
—meaning us—-
as if there were somewhere else.

THE SIBLINGS

Once upon a time, there were three brothers and three sisters. And because their father was a king and wished to test them, or their mother a queen who wished them to find suitable mates, or their father had stupidly insulted a witch, or their mother had with a little bent man made a fatal compact. Or because the parents, selfish beyond measure, had tearfully told the children they could not live another day without something like the Evening Star, or God's own nightingale, or a drop of dew from the Garden of Eden - the siblings set off into the dangerous world, in pairs, and in different directions.

Brimming with self-importance, the eldest brother with curled lip booted aside the ancient crone offering advice by sea-tormented rocks. And the eldest sister scorned the hag, comparing her ravaged face and shrunken body to her own glorious self, so lissome, so statuesque, so sexually dexterous.

And when the second son, ever distracted, his mind on compound interest - zeros marching away into a golden infinity - came upon a little rabbit in a snare crying out for help in perfect if shrill human speech, the practical fellow weighed advantages and disadvantages, then matter-of-factly broke the rabbit's neck, skinned it, and roasted it for supper. But not before the second sister, obsessed with clothes and hygiene, used the bunny for a stepping-stone to free her high-heeled boots from the sucking mud, the little voice ascending from beneath her skirts into a sharp shriek.

But when the youngest of the siblings - tender as peeled wands, guileless as chicks - came upon a gaunt child in the darkest precinct of the forest, the brother poured his every last penny into the cupped hands and joined the homeless, while the sister immediately removed her clothes to wrap them and her own naked body around that chilled little one, thereby smudging her image as modest maid, requisite for royal daughter, royal bride.

And it came to pass that whatever and how much the elder siblings saw and took, all was bitter in their mouths, as if for them the waters of the earth had turned to vinegar, the trees to swaying kelp in a dim, drowned, grotto.

But at the moment the youngest gave all away, the universe shifted and realigned itself so that no matter what misfortunes befell them, no matter what pain or disappointments assailed them, a light would probe every darkness to reach them, the noble light of suns.

For do not those closer to Heaven than we, say, in so many words, *Open your heart until it bleeds, and the tears you shed shall take their place among the stars*?

RAPUNZEL

From the Brothers Grimm
*(You doubt Rapunzel's parents had a witch for a
neighbor? But haven't we all had one of those, or the
equivalent? At least we called them that. And what is a
witch, anyway? Maybe just a very sharp woman with no
interest in settling down. And who can do magic. And
what is magic? For a stab at a definition, please look over
the little piece called, interestingly enough, "Magic,"
included in this very volume.
Incidentally, "Rapunzel" is the German word for a kind
of – you guessed it – lettuce.)*

Rapunzel's mother lusts for the lettuce
studding the witch's lush yard
beside their own scribble of weeds.
She's pregnant and persistent
and a general pest
the bigger she gets.

Though driven crazy, hubby
won't ring the neighbor's bell
to ask a favor.
She was never seen,
you see,
and only talked about in whispers.

He climbs the fence.
He steals a head,
greener than nature,
sweeter than sex.

But one salad won't do it
for the addict.
He must steal again for a fix.

So over the fence

he goes in the dark.
But this time
like a bat,
the witch attacks.

"Please!" he pleads. And the response?
"Relax,
I won't kill you
or turn you into something
to be stepped on. In fact,
take all you need
to calm the hysteric.
Only, I want the infant."

And he agrees!
Because he tells himself
she's kidding
"Yeah, sure," he thinks
with a chuckle.
"Just come by
and we'll have her
wrapped up and ready!"
After all,
what can the crone want with a kid?
Did she go soft all of a sudden?
Will a monster
change a diaper?

Thus stopping dead the horrors in his head.
In other words
like most of us
he is small, terrified,
and in denial.

The witch does take the child,
tearing her from her mother's arms,
but never harms her.
Named Rapunzel,
locked in a tower, the girl

learns to sing and comb her hair
which she never cuts.
She's also gorgeous
but doesn't know it,
there in a slot in the stone
fifty feet off the ground.

Enter a Prince
hunting in the woods,
hearing a bird sing. Or is it
a woman! Drawn to the prison
he's dazzled by her mane,
hung nine fathoms to the ground.
Then disgusted by the hag in black
who shows up
and swarms up it
like a louse, but in one hour
slithers down and splits.

Now's his chance!
He advances and hisses,
a witch imitator.
He's a good actor.
"Rapunzel, Rapunzel,
let down your hair!"

And O
it spills like white wine! He climbs it
and fills the window with his lithe self
scaring the hell out of the virgin
who has not lately seen a human
who's not a bent witch. Far from it,
this boy is a knock-out (what else?)
with a smooth line.
In an hour she's his.
They agree to run.

But how to get down?
The prince will return that a.m.,

and they'll use sheets,
nothing unique.

But the witch re-enters,
and with x-ray vision
sees Prince-prints all over the girl
and attacks, Rapunzel banished
to a scowling swamp,
her tresses snipped,
the boy to be dealt with
like this:
when he reaches the window
after climbing the hair
lashed to a hook,
there's ten nails at his face. He falls
to the thorns
and out he crawls,
blind.

For years he drifts in a night
with no moon nor dawn,
groping whatever he bumps
for that perfect nose, that stream
of hair. (Notice,
it took a mere hour for love to bloom.
But remember when you were young.
Time stretched or snapped
like gum.)

Then by the magnet of love,
a voice finds him caught
in branches and roots
like traps, singing of
lettuce and weakness. Rapunzel
in the flesh!

Arms embrace. Tears fall
And believe,
or bore us to death

with common sense: the drops cleanse
the retina, cleanse the lens.
The colors of the world unfurl in the prince
like tint
dripped in black paint. The sun
again stuns him
as does the beaming woman.

Then off to an applauding kingdom, the crowd
needing nobility
for their fantasy,
young beauty to copy,
and an old witch to blame for everything else.

RAPUNZEL'S PARENTS

What about them
after Rapunzel was picked up at birth
by the punctual witch?
The Grimm Brothers are mum.
German bedtime tales
evidently love to keep us guessing.
I love to think up theories based on what I've seen.
I've seen couples cling because of mutual shame.
I mean, who else would have them?
Who else would listen even,
without judging?
Who else but the husband
would say nothing of his wife's
stupid obsession with lettuce,
so dangerous,
he who had ransomed her fetus
to save himself?
He alone.

And so they might have lived
too long in the room
overlooking the Garden of Evil
(now that the witch was gone
no longer jammed with juicy, giant freaks
of the Vegetable Kingdom
like victims of radiation,
but thick with thorns as cruel as guilt),

barely looking,
never touching,
hardly breathing.

FRIAR TUCK

(...was of course a member of the legendary Robin Hood's band, those who stole from the rich to give to the poor. (Oh, may they reappear tomorrow!) Here's how the monk might have explained himself.)

I never hit a target, never reached one, actually. I'm too fat for archery. My attempts planted short woods of thin trees with bright feathers from my toes to the target. So I became the priest of Sherwood Forest, giving what I did have to give. I heard the confessions of thieves. I placed the sacred wafer on all those forked tongues. I made the Sign of the Cross at holes in the ground when the boys were too slow around the Sheriff's men. And I had no church but an arch of oaks, no diocese besides miles of woods that no man with money would enter without an army. Unless he himself was running from the executioner's axe.

When the king put a prize on Robin's head, a true man whose heart bled for the beggar, the bard, the mother - right then I gave up my sweet bed and the silken delights of rich churches. Right then I began to live the Life they play-act on altars.

PONCE DE LEON

Inspired by William Carlos Williams' In The American Grain

(Let us sail into more recent times, acknowledging that the creation of fairy-tales and myths didn't stop with the Middle Ages. American so-called history crawls with them. Think of Washington and the cherry tree. Lincoln walking ten miles to return a penny to a customer.

These may have been actual historical events, though as in all things, there are varying opinions about that. But more important, these stories and a thousand others become fixed in what is known as our national narrative, the mythology that we share that helps bind us together as a vast political unit. Take our boy Ponce, for instance, the Spanish explorer who raped Puerto Rico in the 15th Century.

As with everything else, I've taken some liberties. This is a free country, ain't it? Ain't it?)

The old goat weds a young girl
from a good family with money troubles.
He enjoys showing her off to his cronies.
"Look at her and weep," he wheezes
behind a cigar
as she glows in the gloom of his
Caribbean mansion
built by Indian slaves,
a light in a cave.

At night if he hasn't drunk too much
he takes his pound of flesh,
not caring if she lies as stiff as a stick,
her lips a slit,
so lovely is she to look at
that skin,
that hair like smoke smudging his sheets.

One night, his rooms jammed with plunging necklines,
stuffed shirts, blazing candles,
and sweating Indians in stupid vests
to make them look like servants
instead of objects,
puffed-up Ponce
orders his wife to play the lute, yelling,
"Alright, people! Shut up and listen
and die of envy!"

The girl touches the thing.
The strings tremble like fawns.
Sweet songs flutter in the cigar smoke
eager to escape.
And two things take place:
the crowd of drunks and their wives
actually do shut their mouths.
And Ponce sees that his wife
is better than he is.
He thought he was buying a piece of ass
when what he got was a princess.
Only class could quell that audience.

Now helpless,
he dies when she twists from him
and burns in hell when he tries it still,
but there's nothing at the tip of him
but him,
stuck in her.
She's elsewhere on some green hill
outside his halitosis.

He kneels at an altar.
"I know it's out of character,
Oh, Lord,
but I fell in love with my wife.
Who won't look at me twice. Ah,
if I could only be young

and slim, and start again
with anything but genocide,
something kind,
so that she would smile
and touch me in public!
Oh, Jesus, on your nails!
For you the dead climbed out of holes,
the lepers leaped, and the blind gaped.
So is my prayer that selfish?"

Now the squaw in the gloom has him!
She'd been waiting in the shadows for years.
What better way to avenge her children,
made slaves,
than drop the hint of a drink
that can melt the years and free the kid
trapped in old bastards,
even capitalists,
to skip again in the sun?

Poor Leon!
That's all he needs!
Maddened by the elusive one,
ready to reverse time in her direction,
ignoring all advice,
sailing north through waves by the million,
harsh dawns, soft sundowns,
nations of pelicans,
flying fish,
he drops off the map to a hot coast,
low, muttering.

It sucks him in, him and his men.

After weeks of mosquitoes, nights of drums,
days of snakes, spiteful vines,
no Fountain, no Youth, but eyes
stalking them through the palms,
they slump into a swamp and sink and choke

except for Ponce who has the spunk
of a wild old man in love with youth
driving him back to the cross of life
long after life has had enough.

He rips his face from the mud.
His eyes light when they hear a lute.
He looks for a pale shape in the shade
he prays is his wife,
naked, smiling, and open to him at last
at the stroke of death.
But a bird flutters
on the wet palm of a palm-leaf,
repeating those lute-like notes.
And an arrow nails the old man's mind shut.

TURKEYS AT THANKSGIVING

(Speaking of fairy-tales, those they teach our school-children as history would be laughable, if it didn't create such obedient little soldiers willing to sacrifice their precious lives all too often for the benefit of the power elite. Here we have one such historical incident that is made myth by leaving out the nasty stuff that came after. I mean, how many K-12 students hear about the ethnically cleansing Pequot War of 1637?)

Now turkeys roam our woods and fields
by the millions.
Some angel brought them back from extinction.
I see them moving through the brush as if the place
belonged to them and always did.
Which it did.
But these are not the fat idiots
lined up in the death-houses.
These are lean and sharp as arrowheads.
You cannot sneak up on them.
They have the eyes of birds, ears of dogs.
Just think wrong, they're gone.

They say the Pequots saved the Protestants
with turkeys on the granite coast that winter.
A generation later, those religious nuts
erased the Pequots
with the usual European efficiency.
But that's history.
Let's stick with myth at least today.
Let's have the Indians and the Christians sitting down
side-by-side at a wooden table piled high
with turkeys, yams, berries, and all the trimmings.
All present are grinning.
Myth is good for your digestion.

Oh, and one more thing.

I hear that turkeys in the wild have attacked people.
Gobble! Gobble! Gobble!

SUPERMARKET TRAGEDY

(Let's look around in our own time, shall we? I'm reaching with this one, I know. I'm including it with myths and fairy tales because it mentions a certain mischievous baby and an ideal, mythical landscape. But also because, as Joseph Campbell has reminded us, we can find myth unfolding in our own lives. Of course. Since we humans create myths and fairy-tales, their elements must be present in us.

Pretty slick, eh? You can see I went to college. But the most important reason this piece is here, is because I got such a kick out of writing it.)

When he fell hard
for a cashier at the Safeway
he haunted the place,
boiling with hormones
and attention-getting schemes.

He talked a mile-a-minute,
laughed with a crack in his voice,
even tripped strategically
with a crash,
dripping real blood.

She barely looked up,
in the green uniform that inspired all this
in the victim -
the cling,
the hang.

He used the snob ploy - bok choy, goat-cheese -
hoping she'd realize
what a hip dude it was
strutting before her,
peeling his wallet.

Forget it.
He had to stand there
and watch her ogle the clock,
chatter with her colleagues,
and finger a thousand things
except our prince,
slinking to his bloated kitchen,
sickened by food stinks.

Still, love drove him back to Safeway
where he danced
symbolically to the counter
with a can of tomato paste
as a crushed heart,
the next day an apple, fruit of sin,
and then in a fit,
a carrot!

She remained distant.
And corporate.

Ah, Cupid!
You could have shot him
in some nice scenery at least. You know,
trees, a stream, a white temple
in the misty distance.
But no. He swooned
beneath buzzing fluorescents
in the department of meat
to the thumping and screaming
of the bubble-gum junk
we're forced to listen to
on the sound systems of supermarkets.

VERY OLD AND HOLY

(This is an experience of mine, another example of how myth and its mysteries are still very much with us, despite the laws against them handed down by the sterner priests of Scientism.)

I bought the old guy a drink when I caught him brooding over an empty glass. During a lull in the jukebox onslaught he said, "You seem like a ok feller. In the same business I used t' be. So I'll give you some free advice. When you're raisin' walls? Look at every stud first and try and see which way the knots is beveled at. That'll be toward the bottom of the tree they come out of. And that's the manner you want to install them studs. Right side down. Right side up. That's how the tree stood alive and that's how you want to stand the parts of 'er. That way you'll be makin' a happier house. Less trouble. I kid you not."

Suddenly resurrected by money, the jukebox exploded again and the old guy started on his stool and stared around the bar, which, with its glacier of smoke, blurry faces, stale air, and clamor, brought to mind a stricken submarine.

"I know why," he shouted over the thump and bellow. "But I just can't say it in here. Very old and holy, though. And right as rain."

DOPPELGANGER

(This lovely German word refers to the ghostly twin of a living person, who may appear now and then, or finally at or near the hour of death.)

When he reached antiquity
he saw that he had spent his whole adult life
hiding from his real self,
bricking it up to kill it,
so to speak,
like that guy in Edgar Allan Poe's story
who gets the man he hates drunk as a skunk,
leads him laughing into the cellar,
chains him laughing still to the wall,
then calmly mixes a heap of mortar
and builds a solid cell around the drunk
who sobers up and begins to scream
and screams until his voice is finally stilled
when the last brick is laid
and the killer walks away
into the lovely night air.

That's Birthday Boy
except his story doesn't end there.
His guy behind the bricks doesn't die
but waits years for the chains to rust away
and the mortar between the bricks to rot
so that he can stagger into the fugitive's umpteenth
birthday party he is throwing with his TV and his cat,
and in a raspy voice after a zillion years of damp, croak,
"So, let's see...
where were we?"

THE DEAD OF WINTER

(Here's another example of the myths among us today.)

For a moment Mrs. Bindshedler felt the house rushing upward through a billion bone-white stars toward a black nothing, and her head swam. But it was only heavy snow falling down past her window. It was only bare branches scraping her wall. It was only Mr. Bindshedler three hours late, at night, in the dead of winter.

Mrs. B. looked away from the window and back toward the faces on the tv screen, which for three hours had talked about everything in the universe except Mr. Bindshedler and his present position in it.

By the fourth hour she switched off the tv and sat completely still.

By the fifth hour she saw clearly that the house and everything in it was dead matter. Only she and Mr. Bindshedler were alive.

Or was he? She leaned her head against one of the hundred little Dutch girls on the wallpaper and pulled her housecoat down over her thin cold legs.

Then a car pulled into the driveway, very slowly. She hopped to the window and looked. The car was a cube of snow being snowed on. Then the side of it split open and a bundled person came out and trudged to the front door. Mrs. B. flung it open.

It was Mr. Bindshedler, but a deeply serious Mr. Bindshedler. He stood under the exterior light which had burned for him since six p.m. and whose wan cone of light was choked with falling white feathers.

"I have some very bad news for you," Mr. Bindshedler said in a soft but perfectly clear and sober voice. "Please be brave. Your husband fell from the ferry tonight and was drowned. No one saw it but me." Then, after a pause, "He was, of course, inebriated."

Mrs. Bindshedler peered at the old familiar face. "Then who are you?"

"I am...was his guardian angel," was the reply. "On occasion we take on the appearance of our clients."

The snow blew in through the open door. Mrs. B. shivered and hugged her housecoat. "Well, you didn't do a very good job guarding him, did you?"

Mr. Bindshedler's angel slumped in his coat and bowed his head. "I've never been very good at anything," he muttered. The white feathers of snow were building up on his head and shoulders, trying to bury him.

"Neither was Mr. Bindshedler," sighed Mrs. Bindshedler. "Well...sir...can I offer you a coffee at least? How do you take it? Cream? Oh, wait. I don't have cream. Milk ok? And do you take sugar or Sweet 'n' Low?"

The snowman raised his Mr. Bindshedler head. "I like it the way he liked it." And he lurched in through Mrs. B.'s doorway, stamping his shoes for a full minute on her Welcome mat.

"Well, close the door, will you Fred, I mean sir?" Mrs. B. took his coat and hung it with the rest of Fred's coats.

"Please sit down!" she called to him over her shoulder. "Please don't just stand there! Oh, that chair there! That's where you, he always sat!"

Finally there came a moment when Mrs. Bindshedler and the angel looked into each other's eyes across the kitchen table. Mrs. B. immediately dropped hers. They burned. They hadn't been that intimate with any man's eyes in years, not even Mr. Bindshedler's.

"Are you sure you're not Mr. Bindshedler?" she asked, just to say something. She had not yet, she realized, even approached coming to grips with all that happened and was continuing to happen.

The angel shook his head. "Humans need to be sure about things, whereas we angels are not sure about much at all. That's alright with us. We've come to accept that the truly important things are beyond understanding."

They ended up in the bedroom with the tropical lamp-shades and the silvery wallpaper. Because when Mrs. Binshedler had picked up the angel's empty coffee cup, she couldn't resist stroking his bald head, identical to her husband's. But unlike her husband, the angel had reached up and pulled her mouth down to his. His kiss tasted of snow and pine-needles.

Feeling his emptiness and strange coolness in her arms, Mrs Bindshedler spent the night trying to fill the angel with all the warmth she had. And he responded with a gratitude that caused to her cling to him in the darkness with all her strength.

Toward the dawn the angel whispered, "The universe is very lonely."

Mrs. Bindshedler began to sob.

"What is it, dear one?" asked the angel.

"I believe you now. I believe you are...what you say you are, and that Fred is really gone and I'm alone."

After a moment the angel murmured, "I'm here."

"But why? Why did you come to tell me about Fred? I know it isn't usual."

After an even longer moment the angel answered, "Because I've been in love with you for years – an angel in love with his client's wife. Can you believe it?" He sighed. "I just couldn't bear your never knowing, your being unable to make a new life with a clear conscience. But I...I did not anticipate this. Thank you."

Mrs. Bindshedler stopped sobbing. They fell asleep.

In the harsh light of a snow-filled morning, Mrs. B. reached for the angel and found he was gone. She leaped up with a cry and ran to the front of the house. There he was in the kitchen boiling water.

"I'll make coffee for us. Then I must go," he told her.

Mrs. B. stood next to the person in her kitchen who looked exactly like her deceased husband but certainly did not behave like her deceased husband, God rest his irritable, pickled soul.

"Go where?" she asked, looking into the angel's lustrous eyes. "Back to the guardian business? You're really not very good at it, are you? And I get the impression you're not so happy doing it either. Am I right?"

The angel turned his back to her and looked out the window at the still-falling snow. The car had become a round white bump on a flat white world.

"But," Mrs. B. murmured to the back of his neck, "there is something you do very, very well. So why don't you stay with me and cultivate your talent? We all need something to be proud of."

Mr. Bindshedler's angel remained at the window. The clock on the wall with the broken cuckoo permanently sticking out of it ticked. Mrs. B. held her breath.

Finally the angel turned, shaking his head. Mrs. B's heart sank. But there was a crooked smile on the angel's face, the first she witnessed, but not the last. Her heart resurfaced.

"You really are something, my dear," said the angel through his grin. "You really are a treasure. Well, it's stilll snowing. I'll stay until it stops."

But the angel stayed with Mrs. Bindshedler for the rest of her life, allowing himself to grow old as she did. The day after she died, he took the ferry and was never seen again.

But that was not to happen for many happy years. At first the couple's friends and the folks at the office were astounded by the change in Mr. Bindshedler, suddenly calm and friendly and sober. But they got used to it and came to trust him and depend on him for affectionate sympathy and good advice.

When Tiff Bindshedler came to visit her parents the following Christmas, she was stunned by the amount of touching her parents managed to fit into their waking hours, and the youthfulness of her mother, and the new-found sensitivity of her father, a man who now listened carefully to what she had to say and who drank one glass of wine at dinner and no more.

At last Tiff was able to speak to her mother alone. Mother and daughter stood close together in pale daylight in the kitchen. Mrs. B. listened to the young lady's questions with luminous eyes, but uttered only a few words in return.

A week later, Tiff told a strange tale to her co-workers in the courtyard of a metallic restaurant in San Francisco's Financial District.

"Well," she drawled, with a pair of sunglasses perched on her severely-chopped hair. "You can't imagine how *weird* it *was*! My parents have turned into to hot lovers! And when I managed to pry them *apart* and cross-examine Mom, know what the only thing she said to me *was*?" Here Tiff imitated Mrs. Bindshedler's small, earnest voice. "It was an *angel* who brought the warmth back into *this* house, an angel out of the *snow!*"

And all of the young people, sitting in their coats in the thin winter sunshine, rolled their eyes and ordered desert and spent the rest of their lunch- break discussing the weirdness of parents and the endlessness of Eastern winters and their great good fortune in escaping the whole business.

UNCLE SUNNY

(Let's make up a myth. I know part of the standard definition of "myth" is that it's a story with no known author. So sue me. Or us. Let's make up a myth about the Sun. It's been done before, of course. The Aztecs and the Mayans come to mind. And the Ancient Egyptians and the Ancient Greeks. But let's make up a fresh myth about the Sun, using the formulae of the ancients – that is, to attempt to get our minds around the cosmic by changing the universe into something humans are familiar with. Remember Apollo hauling the Sun around the sky in a horse-drawn chariot? How wild is that!)

Uncle Sunny was born in the Big Bang.
Things jammed so tight
they blew Uncle and the other suns to twelve midnight
in the night that ends never, period,
where they crackled and glared,
boring him.
He was a special sun with sex-drive and vision,
not about to spend Sundays
sunning himself and smoking cigars
while his buddies hissed and popped in the dark
like dumb atomic match-heads
setting fire to themselves
forever.
No.

So he tried sex with his family,
dead mostly,
but the nearest bodies.
Though only with the girl called Earth
did he connect.
Her lucky muck twitched
spawning a baby called Life,
horny the next minute.

It's been a good arrangement.
Never mind the incest.
It happened before the rules were set.
You can blame it on boredom.
On one hand there's the Universe,
the flying graveyard.
On the other there's Life
banging through bodies
by the billions
that change like clouds.
Now that's interesting.

So the couple can chuckle as they sail toward nothing.
And Baby plays.
And the Universe
has a reason to fly,
since without Life it's just
rocks and room,
and beyond the rocks
more room,
and...

I surrender.
The priests can shrink it to an opera
with a king on a throne.

I just walk in the sun
while I'm able.

THE PERSONALTIES OF NUMBERS

(Do numbers have a place in myths and fairy tales? You bet. The Twelve Labors of Hercules. The Seven Dwarfs. The Three Wishes. Numbers are everywhere. Obviously, they fascinate the creators of these stories, whether they are poets or ploughmen. In fact, lots of people in lots of places believe that numbers are more than mere symbols of quantity - they also have magical powers. I don't know about that. But looking at numbers as they simply lie on a page, I suddenly, in a "magical" moment, saw what might just be their individual personalities. I know, I know. Just bear with me.)

1 is proud of its place at the head of the column,
ever at attention
feet aligned
nose in the air.
But in private 1 is glum,
worth less than the rest
to anyone.

2 is happy.
2 is married
and knows how to get along. 2
never sleeps alone.

Everybody loves 3, 3
is pretty and poised.
But 3 has three tips
that never touch.
So 3 is innocent.
3 is a virgin.
3 is religious.

4 is dangerous.
4 is relentless.
You can cut yourself on 4.

Add three lines and
a swastika blooms.
4's room is very neat.

Dazzle the world with a smile!
is 5's motto.
5 has a sunny aspect
and a pompadour
and an ample bosom.
But 5 would sell you anything.
Watch out for 5.

6 is nothing much itself
but a cousin to 9,
another non-entity.
But 6 is pregnant
with possibility.
6 is pregnant.

Svelte from birth.
Good stock there.
Always wins.
The dice roll right for 7.
But since 7 never suffers, 7
can be as cruel as a striking snake
which it resembles.

Ah, poor 8!
8 has eight kids.
8 works from eight to eight.
8 drinks beer
and has a lousy figure.
But altogether
8's the salt of the earth.

9 is nervous
looking off to the distance,
anywhere away from the
attention of 10.

And what is 10?
10 devours all of them!
has a brilliant future
of zero after zero until the end.
10 is male and female.
10 is a pine and a lake.
10 is up and down and all around.
10 might be everything.

HAMADRYAD

(Here's yet another example of myth coming alive nowadays. This all really happened to a close friend. I've changed nothing.)

The trail was dark when he walked into the woods, but in a short time the moon came out to light up the ceiling of mist just over the treetops. Between that and the dull reflection of the mist off the snow, he was able to see well enough the black oak trees marching away from him on every side. Their naked winter branches, clicking in a cold sea-breeze, crisscrossed against the faint sky,.

He had been alone too much lately, but there he was alone again. Only in the woods, his old refuge, it didn't feel as bad.

After a half-hour's walk, still alone, still seeing no one nor anything at all besides trees, snow, and bitter winter sky, he came across a wreck in the woods. A tall oak lay across the trail at the height of his hips. He could see the round pedestal of roots and frozen earth tilted straight up where the tree had been ripped out of the ground – by a hurricane, of course. They happen in the fall around there.

Just before him was a section of its trunk, bare of branches. He'd just slip one leg over it, then the other, and he'd be on his way.

But as he moved up to the horizontal tree through the dim light, it began to take on the appearance of something impossible. And when he placed his hands on it to shimmy over, the illusion, if that's what it was, became unmistakable.

It was as if he had rested his palms on the belly of a human woman, just a few inches above her Mound of Venus, beyond which a pair of incredibly long, perfect legs stretched away into tangled branches, then darkness.

Of course, he only had to glance up to see oak after oak swelling at some point above the ground, then splitting off into two main branches. But when I looked back down on his tree – on her – gleaming dully in the wan light like flesh, he saw a fallen tree to be sure, but at the same time the voluptuous torso of an elongated goddess, or at least an awfully suggestive sculpture of one. Nature had chosen to recreate a woman in wood, or his lonely imagination had.

At that moment he never minded which. She represented something he sorely lacked. More, in that lonesome highly-charged place, with its tricky moonlight screened by a thousand swaying branches, she almost *became* that something, as if a real woman were trapped inside the tree, her fierce struggle to get out swelling through the bark, shaping it from within to her own figure.

Without thinking, he began to caress the tree as he would a woman, which excited him, not in a sexual way exactly, although his hands were happy enough to roam female hills and valleys again, cold bark and all. It was the perversity of it! A man in a dark wood stroking a tree!

It felt sinful. There *are* laws of nature.

But it made him happy.

To his surprise, it also made him stiffen a bit beneath his overcoat as he leaned up against her, his hands stroking and kneading.

Half-amused, half-scandalized by his own behavior, he did what he might have done if this had been a more conventional situation. He lowered his head to give her loins a long, gentle kiss. Her bark there was smooth and thin, his cold nose detecting a tangy hint of pitch, his lips sensing – life! And it struck him that a few of her roots might still reach into the earth, might still, slowly, slowly, squeeze sap up her veins, but that nevertheless she was dying, surely dying.

Genuine sorrow for her filled him.

But then he jerked up. He heard a cough from the surrounding trees! Small, dry, but a cough!

He turned in a circle at the side of his tree, his heart stalled, his face hot. What if someone had seen…!

He stared hard down the avenues of black tree trunks in pale snow that all ended in darkness. But detected no movement at all other than the slow sway of trees and the twirl of dead leaves on a branch or two.

Then he remembered that the parking lot of the State Park had been empty of cars when he pulled in, and that it was a Sunday night in January.

There were no humans in those woods other than himself. He was certain of it. As for the cough? Trees made strange noises, especially in winter when their leaves were gone and nude branches rubbed each other. He had heard other winter woods squeal and groan as if nails were being pulled.

He waved it away. It was nothing. He began to breathe again.

But the sharp noises had been enough to wreck his romantic mood. As lovely as his lady tree yet looked in her open-legged arch, his love-making was done for the night. Anyway, his feet were wet. He'd go home with plenty to think about. He gave his wooden lady a wistful final stroke and started back.

A dozen steps down the dim trail he heard the cough again and whirled around. In this night of shocks, he was to have one more - the Grande Finale.

A dozen satyrs crossed the trail between his lady and him at a quick trot, their hooves thumping the snow – but satyrs without heads or torsos! What he saw were trotting pairs of legs that bent backward, topped by naked rumps, each rump wearing a white, pointed cap!

The things were barking angrily, undoubtedly explaining the coughs. But he felt more shock than fear. Although he sensed a great deal of anger in these creatures, for some reason he didn't believe he'd be menaced in any way, and wasn't.

Now the little Rational Man in his mind leaped to the rescue, chalk in hand, Professor Von Logick, the same who had tugged on his sleeve as he made love to the oak, whispering, *It's just a fallen tree, for God's sake!* and *After all you've been through, you fall for optical illusions?* And as for what our friend was staring at round-eyed at the moment, the so-called "satyrs," explained the Professor with a hint of scorn, *These are nothing more than the gleaming rear ends of Eastern White-tailed deer, who are loudly letting you know just how annoyed they are at your wandering around in their woods at that late hour. The darker front sections of their bodies are simply invisible in the murk. Understood? Case closed.*

Ah, how comforting are rational explanations! They wave away mystery as we would an irritating insect! And as a product of this techno-scientific society of ours, in which science is the latest religion, our friend felt that almost silly relief he always felt when the voice of reason clicked on in the darkest, scariest of nights, and he was assured that *it* was only the wind, *it* was only a dream, *it* was only the product of a feverish imagination.

Even that night he was actually able to smile sheepishly in the frigid darkness after the Professor's reassurances. Still, he looked over his shoulder plenty walking out of those woods, since the herd of whatever they were, though invisible again, coughed from the shadows on either side of him as if to let him know he was being escorted the hell out of there, he had better believe it.

But reassurances aside, this business in the East Coast winter woods so haunted our hero that three weeks later and two thousand miles to the west, he found himself telling the tale to a brainy friend, telling it as he would a joke – a joke on him.

"I actually believed," he chuckled, "or half-believed for a few minutes that what I was feeling and seeing was…well, unexplainable, supernatural, weirder than hell, anyway…" He had expected her to readily agree with the rational explanations. She too, after all, was a product of our techno-scientific society. He was wrong.

"My friend! My dear friend!" she cried, taking him by the shoulders. "You are twice-blessed! You got to make love to a Hamadryad and walk away in one piece!"

"A what?"

She opened a dictionary of classical mythology to a certain page and placed in our boy's hands. He read:

Hamadryad. Greek. A nymph who lives in an oak tree and dies when the tree dies. Some times the consort of satyrs.

"What a coincidence!" he had stammered.

But, he told me years later, for an instant, as if through parted drapes normally tight shut, he saw trees clothed in green, swaying in a summer breeze. From each of them sang the voice of a woman so that the soft air was filled with glory. And beneath those voices whirred a soft percussion played by invisible creatures stirring in the undergrowth, that may or may not have been locusts.

A FABLE FOR LOUDMOUTHED POLITICIANS

(A fable is defined as a story using animals to illustrate a moral. I don't remember where this one came from. Maybe from nowhere)

One day a fly buzzed down to a pile of manure on a stable floor and gorged on it, stuffing herself to the gills. But when she tried to fly off she found she had taken on too much weight and couldn't rise into the air no matter how hard she flailed her wings.

Noticing a shovel leaning against a wall, she took heart.

"I'll climb up it," she thought, "then launch myself at that great height. I'll be airborne again!"

It took an hour for her to drag her engorged body up the length of the shovel, but she did manage to reach the top. She took a deep breath. She leaped. She beat her wings. She fell straight to the floor and cracked open like a raw egg.

MORAL: *Do not fly off the handle when you know you are full of shit.*

HIGH NOISE

A One-Act Play

(Dear Reader, if you've come this far with me, you deserve a medal, for...what? Courage? Patience? A strong stomach? Yes, to all of these. Unfortunately, I'm fresh out of medals, but at least I can leave you with a happy ending. Seriously, I have enjoyed your company more than you'll ever know)

Characters: First and Second Dryad, The God and Goddess, First and Second Angel, Satan

A bare stage except for a few large rocks. Muted light. In the background a tall iron fence with a gate locked shut by chains. Characters wear simple robes in the classical style except where otherwise indicated, though the time is now.

(Enter First and Second Dryads)

FIRST DRYAD

Has it been two-thousand or three-thousand years we've been prisoners in this place that isn't quite a place, but rather nowhere, nothing? Can you imagine losing track of something like that?

SECOND DRYAD

Natch, sister! Why not, when there aren't any seasons here, and time floats like smoke with no beginnings and no endings? It can drive you nuts...!

FIRST DRYAD

No seasons and no sun, no constellations even, and no Moon either, with her influences on the seas outside us and the seas within.

SECOND DRYAD

And no trees which is the worst for me, now that we're going all weepy again. It's for them more than anything I add to the water-table around here with my tears. It's for those tough old trunks we were born in and would have lived long, laid-back lives in if we hadn't been torn out of 'em.

FIRST DRYAD
Ah! Ah! To breath once more beneath those flowing flags of leaves! To sing with the wind in branches again! To touch, just touch those trunks...!

SECOND DRYAD
Sis, that's enough! I've already beat myself over the head a million times with those memories, and they hurt as much now as ever. Especially when you spice 'em up with all that poetic jive you picked up in High-falutin' Writing Workshop, One and Two. And anyhow, I'm mulling over something besides you or me...

FIRST DRYAD
Which is? And by the way, exactly what do you mean by "high-faluting...?"

SECOND DRYAD
(Waving the First Dryad away with an impatient gesture)
I wonder if Our Lady cries Herself to sleep? I wonder if Her heart bleeds over the trashing of the old ways? I could never tell what She was feeling, not really, not for all these eons.

FIRST DRYAD
You always ask the rude thing! Think the strange thought! Act the wild way! We barely make sense of ourselves. So who are we to analyze the divine mind? To even try? The Universe is a mysterious place and nothing more so than the ocean of thought in gods' heads or the heart that beats in their breasts.

SECOND DRYAD

Ha-ha! Oh, boy! More poetry! I am what I am, sis! Can't help it! But I sure agree about the spookiness of deities. And who could be spookier than the Dude who threw us ladies out? That Man-god who won't allow anybody else to sit alongside Him, except, some believe, his own Son?

FIRST DRYAD

Shush, sister! Your indiscretions will send us downstairs! They say nothing escapes His eyes and ears! And in fact... Oh, my Goddess! Look over your shoulder, sister...! Has He heard you and already dispatched the agent of our punishment?

(The FIRST ANGEL enters, a male in a uniform, and fully-armed.)

FIRST ANGEL

Hail, ladies! I bring you greetings from my Master!

FIRST DRYAD

What a disaster! Sir! Sergeant! Captain! Major! Please forgive my sister! Sometimes her mouth is set loose by something other than her mind....

FIRST ANGEL

I have no interest in you, Miss, or madam, nor do I know what you refer to. But since you are certainly women, the type who lured Adam into his capital offense, I'll wager you're been up to something that could bear investigation. However, for the moment, all that is required of you is that you inform your Mistress that the King of the Universe wishes to speak to Her face-to-face right now, right here.

FIRST DRYAD

You mean, The God wishes to speak with...The Goddess?

FIRST ANGEL

Miss, I said it. Now get on with it. He is expected this minute.

SECOND DRYAD

Sis, why don't you fill our Mistress in on this visit, the first
in three thousand years at least, while I stay and entertain the gent in
the cute uniform?
>(Exit FIRST DRYAD, gladly)

FIRST ANGEL
I do not require entertainment. My mind dwells on a higher plane.

SECOND DRYAD
Uh-huh. Come to think of it, your Master and His Boys ain't exactly a
barrel of laughs, are they...?

FIRST ANGEL
How dare you, woman, speak of the Supreme Being in that tone!
>(Flourish of trumpets)
But wait...Now here is The Very God to speak for His Very Self!

>(THE GOD enters wearing a mask, accompanied by the
>SECOND ANGEL, similar in appearance to the FIRST
>except for a pair of eyeglasses.)

SECOND DRYAD
And here is The Very Goddess to deal with this mind-blowing
situation.

>(Also masked, THE GODDESS enters with the FIRST
>DRYAD. Both GOD and GODDESS tower over
>DRYADS and ANGELS who stand aside as their leaders
>come face-to-face.)

THE GOD
Lady, I greet You. And may I say that though thirty centuries have
driven against Your face and form, nevertheless You retain a certain
purity and comeliness that seem to be fading of late in My Universe.
But come, have You no word of welcome for Your King?

THE GODDESS

Does the prisoner welcome the jailer?

THE GOD

I do not think that analogy is apt here. I am the Supreme Being and have a Master Plan that is beyond the understanding of anyone but Me.

SECOND DRYAD

Evidently.

FIRST DRYAD

Sh-h-h-h!

THE GOD

What is that? Did I hear something from Your crew?

THE GODDESS

Having no trees and no wind to sigh through them, here in this empty place You have placed us in to fit Your scheme of things, my women use words to recreate the world they once played in.

THE GOD

They do not 'recreate' the world, Lady. They cannot since I created the heavens and the earth and only I can recreate them or destroy them. But I sense a bitterness in You. I taste a drop of vinegar. I sniff the whiff of burning leaves. And that is ridiculous and even seditious. Does the rabbit lament her lack of wings?
Does the hawk bitterly crave the dark regions of the rabbit's tunnels?

THE GODDESS

I have heard the rabbit at the impact of the hawk's attack
scream with terror but also rage. All things do not go smiling into the cage of Your will.

THE GOD

And yet, complaints about Me are silly and wasted, since I created all there is and all there will be.

FIRST ANGEL

And against regulations, Master.

SECOND ANGEL

Let them not forget that any complaints are against the regulations. Harsh, perhaps, but that's the way of it.

SECOND DRYAD

I just love men in uniform, don't you?

FIRST DRYAD

Sh-h-h!

THE GOD

For a place with no wind, there is something breezy here.

THE GODDESS

I care nothing for philosophy or theology, these things that men discuss endlessly while the women, with their hands in blood or dirt, give birth and grow corn.

SECOND ANGEL

She's obviously been out of touch for many moons. These days there are women in the boardrooms.

SECOND DRYAD

Out of touch? No kidding! After being hounded out of every inch of the West and beyond? But not before we saw your flag, and only yours, flapping over all Creation. As if the eleventh finger between your legs was holier than the fold between ours, bigger,
so to speak, in the Cosmic Scheme. And then you had the nerve to offer freedom to the woman only if she hid in your shadow and kept her mouth shut. Which we wouldn't do. So you drove us here at

sword-point. You eleven-fingered people are very good with swords, know what I mean?

FIRST DRYAD

Sh-h-h! And sh-h-h! And sh-h-h! times three, sister!

THE FIRST ANGEL

I swear the girl's a witch and should be sizzled!

SECOND ANGEL

Or at least reasoned with.

THE GOD

The wind in this supposedly windless place grows louder. Well, be that as it may, though I have overheard endless hand-wringing and lamentation from Your Dryads all these eons, Lady, I have heard not a sound from You.

THE GODDESS

Lamentation is beneath a god.

FIRST ANGEL

Oh, my God! Arrest them all!

SECOND ANGEL

No matter how crowded anyplace is, there always seems to be more room for the arrested.

SECOND DRYAD

I sense you two have handcuffed a wrist or two in your time.

THE GOD

(thundering)

I am the only god there is!
(The Dryads hold their ears. But not The Goddess, who appears completely unfazed.)

THE GODDESS

Oh no, Sir. I beg to disagree. I do so though You may drive us even further from the earth's beauty - I mean in a downward direction. No, Sir. You would like to think that You can be whatever You like and do whatever You like with no partner to answer to or be unduly concerned about as some people do. That is until they find out too late how bleak it is to boast and bray through life without an opposing opposite lover to grow against - and with. But look here. Do You not see me before you? I am here and I am immortal too, though without a passport at the moment.

THE GOD

(With more thunder, and now lightning)
I am the only god there is!

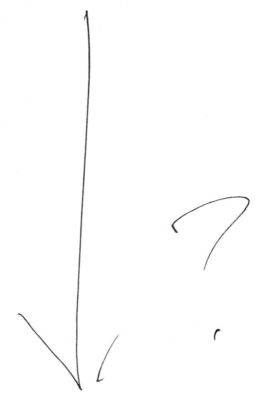

FIRST ANGEL

He is the only god there is!

SECOND ANGEL

What the King says is reality, whether reality agrees or not.

THE GODDESS

(to The God)
Then why are You here?

SECOND DRYAD

Then why *is* He here?

FIRST DRYAD

Are you completely mad? Sh-h-h!

THE GOD

I am here because though we weeded the field, then burned the stubble, and seeded salt in the blackened furrows so that the field lay fallow and silent for centuries, lately rude buds have pushed through the dust as if they had a place in the sun against My will.

SECOND DRYAD

Metaphors make me dizzy.

FIRST ANGEL

How would you feel at the end of a rope?

SECOND ANGEL

That is one way to punish crime. The question is: what is crime? The answer? The acts of those who lost.

THE GODDESS

I believe You speak of those who have rediscovered Me.

THE GOD

Exactly. By some sort of sorcery You have slithered back into Mankind's mind....

SECOND DRYAD

He means Womankind and those other characters.

FIRST ANGEL

One more noise from those rude lips...!

SECOND ANGEL

And doors may close behind you, Miss, that may never open again. Believe me. I've seen them.

SECOND DRYAD

Just like the Inquisition.

FIRST DRYAD

Let us pray those dark days stay locked away.

THE GOD

...slithered back, I say, and too many of My people have turned from My Law and from what I have wrought. And it seems to Me their eyes have slid toward You.

THE GODDESS

And what have You wrought? Trees falling like wheat before the reaper. Water, the blood of the Mother, poisoned. The air tainted by machines, the gleaming contraptions of Your devotees who learned from You that they are superior to Nature and must control her instead of living reverently with her until she takes them back into herself, in the ancient dance of life and death. And even that Your technologists are working to thwart!

SECOND DRYAD

And the ego, Mistress, if I might drop a hint? The gratification of it despite the devastation of everything around it?

THE GODDESS
Ah, yes.... As if there were but one star in the Universe, male in sex, You have shone alone, setting that example to those who raise their eyes for guidance. For what do they see? A man alone running the company. Not a woman nor a family - though in my time I shared my throne with husbands and their relatives and mine. Nor do they find a council of other deities to bring fresh opinions and fresh ideas before the throne. No. Just one solo God with a deep voice. And as it is in Heaven, so it has been on Earth: the most rampant selfishness since the planet's birth.

SECOND DRYAD
Did you hear the way She said that, Sister? I couldn't have said it better.

FIRST DRYAD
And you've had so much more practice at saying things! Now, Sh-h-h!

SECOND DRYAD
You grow wittier as you grow older, dear, though it seems to have taken forever.

FIRST ANGEL
Just give us the order and we'll cuff her and her.

SECOND ANGEL
And their wit will fade like fish slapped on a hot rock.

THE GOD
I see, Lady, You have a list of complaints that must have taken centuries to compile. Now let Me review *Your* case. What did I find when I walked in Your places, Your sacred groves, and hills of vines and temples of smoke and snakes? Sacrifice, human sacrifice, of men,

mostly. But even worse, backwardness lying like a low mist across Your estates, ten thousand years of entrenched habits to do with sticks and clay and the skins of beasts, and slack-jawed superstition that conjured gods and imps and nymphs in every tree, valley and sea - superstition that drew pictures of them in the stars and wove them into the seasons and the healing of sickness. Backwardness so bottomless that people lived and died in a single piece of a single corner of a single place with no interest whatsoever in any other. In other words the human mind was wasted. That bright light I lit in the human skull was working at the level of an insect's or an ox's.

Change was due and I brought it. I showed my children their rightful place in the Grand Plan - on a peak overlooking the entire planet.

SECOND DRYAD
If Your children had simply overlooked "the entire planet" and not ripped her robe off and raped her, then crowed about their "conquest over Nature," we'd have more of a future than we do.

FIRST DRYAD
Sh-h-h, sister! And I'm sick of saying it!

SECOND DRYAD
And I'm sicker hearing it!

THE GOD
Suddenly, the prevailing winds around here offend Me. Men, arrest that woman and take her to a place with nothing whatsoever and no ears to hear it.

FIRST ANGEL
Oh, happiness! Oh, release! Seize her right wrist, brother, and I'll seize the other!

(The ANGELS fasten on to the SECOND DRYAD who struggles against them)

FIRST DRYAD

Run, sister! I'll scratch their eyes out while you hide! At the sight of this outrage I feel a fire inside I didn't know I had!

(The FIRST DRYAD leaps at the ANGELS and is drawn into the fray)

THE GODDESS

(crying out)

Violence! You men forever resort to it! It is because you cannot have babies come out of your bodies that you hurt and kill! There, in the spasm of pain and death is your only contact with the deepest rivers of life - except sex! And even in sex most of you stab instead of stroke!

THE GOD

Witch! To discuss these disgusting mechanics before My chaste face!

THE GODDESS

You are disgusted by surrender and ecstasy and mindless rapture...!

THE GOD

I came to enshrine the human mind, not dim it with sin!

(Enter SATAN in a three-piece suit, razor-cut, and Guccis, through a cloud of his own cigar-smoke. All stop to stare)

SATAN

Yes! Yes! Yes! Yes! I love it, baby! I love it! But do not stop for me! Scratch those eyes out! Rip that hair! Oh, it makes me so happy to see Heaven killing itself I could spit! God against god!
Host against host! All those feathers and halos flying in every direction! Then when your backs are turned, I can conquer the world! Or actually, finish conquering it. Gee, folks, don't look so stunned! I already have a head-start, remember? Look who's running Washington, Beijing, Moscow, London, Damascus, Jakarta, and about every capital in between! Look at capitalism and corporatization and

globalization! And television! I tell you, baby, this is a hostile takeover and yours truly is Mister Hostile in the flesh! So to speak.

THE GOD

It is *you*!

SATAN

You got that right, Daddy-o! And better than ever! (He takes out a cell-phone) Now leave me be for a sec. I gotta to call my favorite exec. She has a question about scratch, natch.

(SATAN dials and speaks aside into the phone)

THE GODDESS

Who is that creature?

THE GOD

Evil incarnate. He was here when You reigned. But though I hate to admit it, grew a bit when I ... well ... took office. My laws being much more numerous than Yours provided that much more sin for him to feed on.

SECOND DRYAD

And notice – the creature is a man!

SECOND ANGEL

But evil comes in more forms than one, Miss. Believe me. I've had to deal with all too many of them.

THE GODDESS

He is an abomination!

THE GOD

(snapping)
I am quite aware of that, Madam! Er...Well...No...You are right. This enemy we have in common. Some action must be taken. Men, arrest him!

FIRST ANGEL

Who, me?

SECOND ANGEL
You mean we two, when You say "men," I assume?

THE GOD
I mean you two when I say "men," unless I am mistaken. But I am
never mistaken! So arrest him!
(The ANGELS release the DRYADS and approach
SATAN from either side, though with considerably less
enthusiasm than they did the DRYADS. SATAN
continues to speak into the phone as he eyeballs them)

SATAN
...know what I mean, lover? Own the water and you own the sucker.
Thirsty people don't argue with the finger on the faucet. But wait. I've
got some flies to swat....

(With a simple martial arts move, SATAN knocks the two
ANGELS to the ground, then continues his phone
conversation)

SATAN
In other words, it's slavery, which is our business plan, ain't it, babe?

THE GOD
He's grown stronger!

THE GODDESS
He did wax ecstatic at our spat.

THE GOD
He gains strength from strife.
(SATAN hangs up the phone and addresses THE GOD)

SATAN
You got that right, Big Guy! For me war is food, holy war a feast. But
I got my big break when You gave the ladies the heave-ho. See, if the
Good stuff is a balancing act - the Golden Mean, the Scales of Justice,

145

yin and yang, and all that jazz, then what's to keep Evil from growing
like a weed when Heaven's out of wack - one Dude running it all,
solo, and the ladies locked up in nowheresville? It was a disaster
waiting to happen, and You're lookin' at the Disaster Master himself!
Ta-ta!

    (Phone rings)

Ah-ha!

> (SATAN speaks into it. Meanwhile, the DRYADS
> whisper together, finally drawing the curious ANGELS
> into their huddle. Then the DRYADS begin circling
> stealthily around the extreme wings of the stage until they
> crouch behind SATAN. The ANGELS move toward him
> as before)

SATAN (cont'd.)

Yeah, General....Of course I knew it was you before I lifted the
phone. I knew it was you before you *lifted* your phone! Think I'm a
fake? Don't make that mistake like so many others who sizzle as we
speak. And I also know the answer to the question you haven't asked
me yet. Forget nuclear, go bacteria. Why waste dough and poison a
place for a zillion years when you could develop it in no time after the
locals are buried? Think shopping malls, housing sprawl, golf-
courses, parking lots right to the horizon-line. Oh, you're worried
about your stock in the atomic industry? Well ask yourself, what's got
a future, the cyclotron or DNA? I told you if it don't pay, dump it. If it
does, hump it…!

    (SATAN looks up at the approaching ANGELS)

SATAN (cont'd.)

And speaking of mutations, I got a couple I need to whack, for good...

> (He is about to dump the ANGELS again, when the
> FIRST DRYAD, so far unnoticed by him, taps him on the
> shoulder. When he whirls around, the SECOND ANGEL
> drops to his knees, the FIRST and SECOND DRYADS
> shove him hard so that he trips over the SECOND
> ANGEL and sprawls on the floor, where the FIRST

ANGEL conks him with his police baton. Then the two ANGELS pick him up and frog-march him to wings of the stage and give him a shove. A long falling cry is heard. The SECOND DRYAD brushes her hands off at a job well done)

SECOND DRYAD
(to the FIRST ANGEL)
You know, you really are an idiot - but not half-bad looking if you'd fix that face. Here! Untie the knots in that forehead of yours! Elevate the corners of your mouth! That's better! Where's a mirror? Boy, are you in for a surprise!

FIRST ANGEL
You confuse me, Miss. But it's not an altogether unpleasant feeling. Something like a glass of beer.

THE GOD
I sense wheels spinning over My head, or great wings beating beyond my understanding, which I thought impossible.

THE GODDESS
But that does not diminish You. In fact it takes greatness of mind to admit that the universe is filled with mystery leading to mystery into more mystery, forever. And so we all must find our way as best we can like starlings in a storm.

THE GOD
I had not thought that anything could lie outside of Me, or that I could be anything but self-sufficient. But this encounter with Your person, so...so surprisingly emotional after all these eons, and the concerted victory that has taken place here, have opened a crack of memory that I had shut tight, of two on a mountain-top, not one, and a warmth not attributable to the sun. Could it be that loneliness has haunted Me, carving Me as a bitter wind would into something harder than I care to admit - without My realizing it? How odd to be unsure! They say that every consciousness is isolated in a prison of the senses. Could

that apply to Mine, though divine? That contradicts the teaching of every great religion in the West, the same, of course, that erased You, You who embrace the Universe as an infinity of mysteries. How intriguing to consider uncertainty as reality....

THE GODDESS

And how humbling. But philosophy is not our cup of tea. I refer to myself and my devotees. And that may be a weakness, as you imply. We may lie too close to the ground and its endless round of life and death to question, investigate, experiment, as Your children have done. Perhaps we've been too earth-bound to climb over custom and discover new ways of healing the body, for instance, or of covering distance even to other earths and moons beyond our wildest dreams, as has been accomplished in Your reign.

THE GOD

As well as ruin, according to You. That may be so. Yes, that may be so. It may be we have risen much too high too fast with too much self-importance. At least in My present state of mind I entertain that notion. But when I am no longer in Your presence (though there is no need for haste in that direction I hasten to assure You) I might have second thoughts.

SECOND DRYAD

Oh, excuse me! Does any of this suggest anything to anybody around here...?

FIRST DRYAD

Sister, let them be! See? They talk to one another, instead of at each other.

SECOND ANGEL

Or past each other.

SECOND DRYAD

...Anything like reconciliation? Negotiation? Cooperation?

FIRST ANGEL

My new... uh...colleague, may I suggest you don't make suggestions to Majesties, whether His or Her Majesty....

SECOND DRYAD

Or both? As in alliance? As in balance? As in the yin on one hand and the yangerooney on the other? As in hooking up, if I can stop beating around the bush?

FIRST DRYAD

Sister, don't rush so! It is enough for the moment that their heads are close and their garments touch. And yet I must admit your vision of double beams of light, male and female sunning the soul, one swelling where the other lacks, yet leaning back for the other's gifts - encourages my budding courage as if father and mother, sister and brother, Queen and King, all lent me some.

THE GOD

(to The Goddess)

Madam, again I hear a wind blowing, but this time strumming a tune so spiced with rich potential, both intriguing and disturbing, that I choose to listen. Lady, would You care to walk with Me a way beneath this music?

THE GODDESS

I cannot think of anything I would rather do, especially if it means stepping foot outside this prison. But upon this one condition: that we look upon each other's inner faces and not the masks plastered on us by the devout and frightened masses who adore us.

THE GOD

Adore Me, at any rate. We have yet to see if they pray to You in an hour of terror. But at least in the matter of our uncovered faces, Lady, I defer to You completely.

(THE GOD and THE GODDESS face back-stage, remove their masks without ever showing their faces to the audience, and exit together, while the SECOND DRYAD and the FIRST ANGEL on one side, and the FIRST DRYAD and the SECOND ANGEL on the other, bow deeply)

SECOND DRYAD
We'd better follow Them or They might lose Their way, entering into new territory or a rediscovered country long neglected.

FIRST ANGEL
Of course my first duty is to attend my Lord. But how much lighter my burden would be with you at my elbow distracting me with your wit and risky thinking! In short, I find the thought of not having you in my hair depressing.

SECOND DRYAD
As homely as your poetry is, I believe it. Can one distrust an old kitchen table or a spoon? And when I take your arm I feel secure. Oh, come or They will disappear, those precious, precious Two!

(The SECOND DRYAD and the FIRST ANGEL exit at speed, arm-in-arm. The FIRST DRYAD and the SECOND ANGEL come to center stage and address the audience together as a CHORUS)

CHORUS
The purpose of this little show was neither to shock nor offend, but to launch a seed upon the wind. Will it find a patch of open mind in which to root? Is that place inside of you? If not, we say go in peace and believe what you will in peace. The world is large enough for as many contradictions as there are nations, though you wouldn't know it for the hatred. But if you are the kind of thinker who will allow a different seed to root and blossom just to see the fruit, to taste it and judge it to be sound or rotten, then tend our tender plant. Tolerate its awkward shape and foreign scent. This might be the day for a different pattern, for a different Eve and a different Adam. Mortals, the gods need you as you need them. All are candles in the wind. Blessings, women, and blessings, men. Oh, Mystery behind everything, bless us all 'til we meet again.

(The FIRST DRYAD and the SECOND ANGEL exit together, hand-in-hand.)

END